the Ellimist Chronicles

Flip the pages to see
the Ellimist . . .

the ELLIMIST chronicles

K.A. Applegate

AN
APPLE
PAPERBACK

SCHOLASTIC INC.
New York Toronto London Auckland Sydney
Mexico City New Delhi Hong Kong

Cover illustration by Romas Kukalis
Art Direction/Design by Karen Hudson/Ursula Albano

ISBN 0-439-21798-9

12 11 10 9 8 7 6 5 4 3 2 1   0 1 2 3 4 5 6/0

Printed in the U.S.A.
First Scholastic printing, November 2000

For Michael and Jake

And for Kelsey Harper

Prologue

The human child called to me. The human child was dying, and nothing I could do within the rules of the game would change that fact.

The human child, one of those who called themselves Animorphs, asked me to explain. In that final moment, the human wanted to know: Was it all worth it? The pain, the despair, the fear. The horror of violence suffered, and the corrupting horror of violence inflicted, was it all worth it?

I said I could not answer that. I said that the battle was not yet done.

"Who are you?!" the child raged. "Who are you to play games with us? You appear, you disappear, you play with us, you use us, who are you, *what* are you? I deserve an answer."

"Yes," I said. "You do. To this question I will give all the answer I know. And when you know me, you will ask another question. And I will answer that question, too. And then . . ."

FIRST LIFE

chapter 1

My full name is Azure Level, Seven Spar, Extension Two, Down-Messenger, Forty-one. My chosen name is Toomin. I like the sound of the word, which is all the reason you need for a chosen name.

My "game" name is Ellimist. Like Toomin, it doesn't mean anything in particular. I just thought it sounded breezy. Never occurred to me when I chose the name that it would follow me for so long, and so far.

The Pangabans were an interesting race well adapted to their unusual world. They lived beneath an eternally gray, clouded sky. They had never seen their own sun clearly, had no notion of stars or other planets. This was particularly ironic because their own planet was in fact a moon that orbited a much larger planet well suited to life.

Had they been blessed with an occasional break in the clouds they might have become a very different race. It is hard to imagine that any species could have lived beneath the sky-filling arc of the main planet, with all its obvious lushness, and not become obsessed with a desire to learn space travel.

But the Pangabans knew nothing of this, nothing at all of anything beyond their own damp and gloomy world.

The Pangabans were six-legged, which is a common enough configuration. They carried their heads high above the slender, muscular body that was little more than a junction of the six long legs.

They were skimmers. Their feet were large, webbed, and concave, which allowed them to walk on the water that covered most of the planet aside from a few soggy islands. They fed by lowering a sort of net from their body down into the water and trolling for microscopic plants and animals of which there was an abundance.

They were intelligent. Not Ketran intelligent, perhaps, but self-aware. They knew who they were. Knew that they existed. Had a language. A culture, mostly involving amazing water dances, feeding rituals, and a religion that centered on belief in underwater spirits that either gave them food or witheld food.

DNA analysis indicated a potential for development. The Pangaban world received a decent dose of radiation, nothing deadly, just enough to cause a respectable rate of mutation. And despite their awkward physiques and the limitations of their planet's natural resources, I believed they could be brought to a level of technology equal to, say, the Illaman Confederation.

There was one possible problem: The main planet around which the Pangabans revolved was populated by an aggressive species of four-legged, two-handed rodents called the Gunja Wave. The Gunja Wave were primitive creatures, only dimly self-aware. But their DNA held promise, too. And their aggressiveness might give them an edge if the two races ever collided.

Still, I had an instinct. I *memmed* my friend Azure Level, Nine Spar, Mast Three, Right-Messenger Twelve. His chosen name is Redfar. His "game" name is Inidar.

"I'll take the Pangabans, if you choose to accept."

"Gladly," he *memmed* back. "You underestimate the value of sheer aggression. You're an idealist, Ellimist."

"Oh? Well, step into my lair, said the *dreth* to the *chorkant*."

Inidar laughed. The laugh worried me a bit. He seemed very confident. But I wasn't going to show him my own doubts. "Shall we immerse?" It was the ritual challenge of the game.

"On the other side," Inidar agreed, accepting the challenge.

7

I checked my real world position, checked to see whether there were any pending *memms* for me to deal with. I didn't want to be interrupted. Then I opened the shunt and was all at once inside the game.

I floated bodiless above the Pangaban world. Drifted above an endless gray-green soup choked with seaweeds and algae and gliding eels that could reach lengths of three miles. I skimmed above one of the mossy islands, brushed one of the squat, stunted, unlovely trees, and found a colony of Pangabans.

The Pangabans were trolling as always, but also playing at something. A game that involved moving in slow, ever tighter circles around one central individual. Not a complex game, certainly not in comparison with the game I played.

Still, I was heartened. Surely an ability to conceive and execute a game was a good sign in any species. It was a gentle, slow, and nearly pointless game, but one that could evolve. Games had evolved on other planets, among other peoples, my own people, the Ketrans, being perhaps the preeminent example.

I wondered what Inidar would do with the Gunja Wave. The essence of the game was minimalism: Do the least thing needed to accomplish a goal.

I knew the least thing. I knew what I would do. A single, simple movement: I would part the clouds and cause the skies to become ten percent clear on any given day. If I had understood fully, if my instincts were correct, that single change in the parameters would launch a revolution among the Pangabans.

I slowed, floated, righted, deployed my wings, and settled down to stand upon the water, invisible to the solemn, slow-moving Pangabans.

I like to feel the texture of the game. I like to be inside it. Only there, only with the alien wind in your wings and the ground beneath your pods (or water, in this case), can you fully know the place. And the place is integral to the species.

I looked up at the unbroken blanket of gray clouds. I couldn't let in too much light or the entire ecosystem would collapse. Just a glimpse.

I felt a thrill of anticipation. The Pangabans were on the verge of an experience they could not even guess at. Their eyes would be opened for the first time. Their universe would expand by a factor of a billion percent.

I smiled. And I *memmed* the game core: Part the clouds.

And the clouds parted.

It was night. The clouds tore apart, a slow, silent

rip. And above the Pangabans the stars appeared. And into that swatch of speckled blackness rolled the planet, all green and blue and orange-scarred.

Slowly, one by one, fearful, the Pangabans did what none of their species had ever done before: They looked up.

They looked up and moaned their gurgling cries.

I heard Inidar's *memm* in my mind. "Shall we accelerate?"

"Fire it up," I answered and *memmed* the game core.

A hurricane! A hurricane of wind and water and earth and time itself. A swirling madness of change. This was the ultimate moment in the game. We had made our changes and now watched time reel forward.

I broke out the displays: DNA mutation, climate changes, technology index, population. For the first two hundred thousand years there was very little change. Then I began to spot the DNA differences in sight and body shape. The Pangabans were selecting for longer range vision, for color vision, for neck length.

And then, all at once, trouble. The algae count was dropping like a stone. It couldn't be! Increased sunlight almost inevitably means an increase in flora. But it was true, the seas were dying.

And then, as I stood untouched amidst the hurricane of change, the first of the carnivore eels emerged to attack the Pangabans. The Pangaban population was decimated in a flash of time.

DNA evolution began to come to the rescue of the Pangabans. They selected for size, downtrending. The smaller were faster, able to evade the eels. Smaller and smaller till the once-towering Pangabans were scarcely larger than one of us Ketrans.

The eel threat diminished. And now at last came the first fluctuation in the technology index. The Pangabans had learned to make a tool. A weapon, of course. A simple spear that could be used to turn the tables on the eels. In short order Pangabans were hunting and eating the eels. Primitive seine-fishers had become true predators.

A million years passed and a very different species now crossed the planet's seas armed with spears and bows. They formed hierarchies dominated by warriors. Their culture shifted ground, favoring a sky god who brought the gift of weapons.

Yes, yes, it was working well enough. Another million years. Perhaps two, and they would learn to move beyond weapons, to . . .

And then, in a flash so sudden it was barely a blip of time, every index went flat. The Pangabans had disappeared. Extinct.

I cursed and heard Inidar's *memmed* laughter.

I reeled back and slowed the playback speed. There it was: The Gunja Wave, still rodentine, but now walking erect, arrived on the Pangaban world in astoundingly primitive spacecraft and promptly killed and ate the Pangabans. They hunted them to extinction and left the planet devoid of its only intelligent species.

"Shall we call the game?" Inidar offered.

I sighed. "What was your move?"

"Oh, a very small one," Inidar said. "I increased their rate of reproduction by a very small percentage. This heightened their natural aggression. And I guessed that your move would be to open the Pangaban skies. Population growth pressures, a limited food supply, and the ability to see the Pangaban surface very clearly . . . my Gunja Wave wanted to eat your species."

"Yes, and they did," I said. "I call the game."

"You have to learn to avoid naïveté, Ellimist. It's not the good and worthy who prosper. It's just the motivated."

"Yes, and you can go surface," I muttered. "See you at the perches for free flight?"

"I'm there, Ellimist."

I shut down the game and opened my eyes to the real world around me.

chapter 2

I am a Ketran. My planet is called Ket. I mention this fairly self-evident fact only because of the plans to open our uninet to visiting off-worlders. The time is coming when a uninet publication may be read by an Illaman or a Generational, not necessarily by Ketrans alone. I don't want to seem chauvinistic.

Off-worlders are usually astounded by the facts of life on my planet. It's fascinating to speak with them because they can give you such a new perspective on what seems so normal to us. The earliest Generation 9561s who arrived to investigate Ket failed even to notice us at first. Oh, they noticed the crystals of course, they weren't blind, but it never occurred to them to look for intelligent life anywhere other than on the planet surface.

The surface of Ket is quite inhospitable to most life-forms, covered as it is by acid seas, lava flows, and strangle-vines. But Generation 9561 (actually they were Generation 9559, then) were gamely wandering around in environmental suits taking samples when one of their air-skimmers accidentally ran smack into a mast of the Great Southern Polar

13

Crystal and a first contact was made that surprised everyone.

Life? On a vast crystal floating three hundred miles above the planet surface? Impossible! But then we'd have thought the same if we'd been the first to arrive on their world and found them down amidst the trees and rivers and so on.

The evolution of my people is obscure. (Interesting how it is often easy to understand the evolution of an entirely different species, and yet be confused by one's own.) Our scientists are confident that at one time we did inhabit the surface of our world, or at least its less sulphurous seas, but at some point the symbiosis of Ketran and crystal was formed and we simply grew together.

Now of course, and for at least the last two million years, we have maintained our symbiosis with the crystals. The age of my own home crystal — the Equatorial High Crystal — has been convincingly established as 1.4 million years. Of course that's half the age of the Seed Crystal, making the EHC one of the newer fully formed crystals.

The term *symbiosis* isn't exactly accurate. We are living and the crystal is not, though it's hard not to fall into a certain romanticism and imagine that it does have something very much like life. What is sure is that we cannot survive without the crystal, from which we derive our sustenance. And it is just as sure that though the crystals can grow without our help, they cannot survive intact long enough to become as vast as they are. The estimates are that a crystal above half a mile in average circumference will crash. The atmospheric pressures and internal buouyancies will lose the battle to gravity at that point. Certainly the seventy-nine-mile circumference of the Seed Crystal is a result of Ketran symbiosis. How would the great crystals continue to float if not for the lift supplied by hundreds of thousands of Ketran wings?

There was all sorts of talk on the uninet about using artificial engines to supply the lift needed for our home. These engines would free us from much if not all dock time. Visionaries talk of how we could go from our current one-tenth free-flight time to as much as one-half free flight. In fact, we would no longer need to maintain stations and fly to provide lift at all. We would only need dockage to eat and rest, while the engines would supply all the necessary lift to keep the crystals afloat in the atmosphere.

But I doubt such an idea will take hold. Deep in our memories we still carry the images, passed down through the millennia, of the terrible crash of the North Tropic Low Crystal. Three hundred thousand years are not enough to erase that memory!

The mere thought made me nervous. I opened my eyes and turned to look downward. Yes, we still floated high above the Eenos lava swamp. No, the ground was no closer than it had been when I immersed in the game. My docking talons were still firmly attached to my niche and my wings still beat their steady rhythm.

Azure Level enveloped me, the sharp, jagged structure of protrusions as familiar to me as the lines of my own hands. Through the smoothed and polished masts, spars, and yards I could see the distant frontier of opaque white spars — the new growth area. I was young, I might be chosen to move into the new growth once it had reached its expected violet hue. Then my name would change. That would be strange. And my ups and downs, my neighbors, would all change, too.

I glanced at Azure Level, Seven Spar, Extension Two, Down-Messenger Forty-two, my closest "up." He was a taciturn person, always had been. I'd tried many times to engage him in the games, but he was a serious scientist, one of those visionaries I mentioned. I thought of him as "Old Forty-two," though I doubt he was much older than me. His chosen name was Lackofa. He pronounced it "LACK-uv-uh." I think it was supposed to be droll.

16

"Hey, Lackofa," I called up, using my spoken voice rather than a uninet *memm.*

His head jerked, causing his rather long and artfully unkempt quills to quiver. He blinked unadorned eyes. He peered around at the sky, as though unsure where the sound could have come from. Finally, slowly, reluctantly, he lowered his magenta gaze to me. "Toomin. What is it?"

"I lost another game."

"Ah. Well, I can certainly understand why you would feel the need to inform me personally of a fact that, were I remotely interested, I could learn from the net."

I wasn't put off by his attitude. Neither of us had ever requested reassignment; that was proof of the fact that we got on well enough as neighbors.

I waited, knowing his curiosity would get the better of him. "All right, why did you lose?"

"Redfar tells me I'm too much of an idealist."

"Mmm. I don't share the fascination with games," Lackofa said. "Any game that can be played can be deconstructed. You can always deduce the laws — assuming you pay attention. And once you know the rules that ensure victory, what's the interest? It's all software. Software is software is software. Boring."

I was peeved at this. It seemed to imply that I wasn't quite bright enough to understand the game. "Alien Civilizations isn't just 'software.' It's the most sophisticated game ever released. It has more than a million scenarios."

"All of which reflect the thought patterns of the game's creators. The scenarios are necessarily limited because the underlying assumptions are limited."

He was right, of course, but I wasn't in the mood to accept his smug judgment. I was in the mood to change the subject. "Are you coming to the announcement?"

"What announcement?"

"What announcement? What do you mean, 'What announcement?' The announcement. Even you know what announcement. They're announcing the nonessential crew for Mapping Crystal Quadrant Three. The EmCee."

"Oh, that. Well, first, I can't imagine why you would feel the need to fly all the way up to the perch when you can know the results almost as quickly on the net. And anyway, I know I'm going."

It took a few seconds for me to register that last statement, spoken as it was in a carefully offhand way.

"You're going? You mean . . . you're going as essential crew?"

"Third biologist," he said, trying out a casual, dismissive wave of his mid-hands that didn't fool me for a second. There was no hiding the pink glow that began at the tips of his quills and spread toward his head.

I was happy for Lackofa. I really was. Except for the part of me that was screamingly jealous. I had a one in five hundred chance of going aboard the Zero-space ship as a nonessential. He had a guaranteed berth as essential crew. We were almost the same age. But somehow he had managed to accomplish a great deal more than I had.

There's a wake-up memm, *Toomin,* I told myself. *Can you read the time cue?*

I was an idiot. I was wasting my life in game playing, free flying, and face-face. Meanwhile Lackofa was on his way into deepest space to see firsthand the things I would see only later, and only on some net sim.

I fell silent. Lackofa didn't seem to notice. Or maybe he just didn't care.

"Well, congratulations, Lackofa," I said, doing a very weak job of ginning up enthusiasm. "That's really an honor."

"Is it? Yes, I guess it is."

I shut up after that. It was wrong to be bitter, but I was. Bitter at myself. I'd steadfastly refused any intellectual specialization. I'd told myself I didn't want to limit my mind by picking one particular discipline. Laziness, that's what it was. I was lazy. I was a daydreamer. I was a juvie at an age when I could easily be taken seriously as an adult. The only thing I cared about was the game, and I wasn't even good at that.

I resolved then and there to change my life. To turn it around in mid-flight. No more nonsense, I had to bear down, I had to grapple, I had to dock-and-hold. I was going to do it: My shunt was going to burn out from the load of educational *memms* I would download. I could do it. I had the brains, I just hadn't decided to get serious.

Okay, well, time's up, Toomin. Make some choices. Make some commitment. Right now. Do it!

Only it was free-flight time. The others would be expecting me. I'd told Inidar I'd be there. Wasn't right to just abandon all my friends just because I'd decided to change.

Free flight first, then I'd explain to my friends that they might not be seeing all that much of me anymore.

chapter 3

The time-cue *memm* popped up and I released my docking talons and disconnected. I felt the blessed silence in my head. No *memms.* No time cues, no updates, no alerts, no "items of interest," no nagging about jobs not done, no urging to examine this or that or the other uninet publication, no guilt-inducing "why don't you perch with us?" *memms* from the dam and sire.

Free flight! I drifted down, down and away from the spar that was my home.

Wings folded back and up, I dead-dived through the masts and spars and rough-hewn new growth protrusions, shot past a swirl-quilled female who cast a languid, unimpressed, but wonderfully turquoise glance my way.

Down and out of the matrix, out into the bare air beyond the reaches of the crystal, out into bare air where I could look down and see the surface clearly. Or as clearly as anyone could, given the yellow, slowly twisting swamp gas clouds down there.

I opened my wings, canceled my momentum,

equalized buoyancy, straining my dorsal intakes a bit as I sucked air.

From here I could get a fuller picture of my home crystal. It's terribly cliché to find it beautiful, but beautiful it was. It filled most of the sky, of course, but even from this distance I could see the generally spherical shape, the ball of brilliant, reflective masts, spars, and yards.

The sun was up and shining bright, and as the crystal moved in a slow rotation the sunbeams blazed, reflected, from a million facets. Ice-blue, palest green, yellow, violet, and pink: It was a lovely sight.

The population was just over half a million now, and at any given time ninety percent of that number would be docked, wings weaving the eternal pattern, providing the endless, tireless lift that kept the crystal from settling slowly to the ground below. The remaining ten percent could be in free flight, if they chose, but in reality it was mostly the younger Ketrans who indulged. Older folks only free flew if they had to commute to some specialized work.

Standing off from the crystal itself, looking like a small moon in tight orbit, the ship: Mapping Crystal Quadrant Three. MCQ3. The EmCee.

It was an omen, perhaps, of our own future, for it looked at first glance like a miniaturized version of the Equatorial High Crystal, except that the spars and masts were clearly not grown and trimmed to form a spheroid, but rather to form an elongated oval with a definite top and bottom. At the bottom the MCQ3 had four massive stems, twice the thickness of a late-growth mast or spar. And attached to each of these four stems was an ugly, thoroughly opaque metal cylinder. These were the Zero-space engines. And they were nothing subversive. The thing that disturbed many people was the much smaller disk located at the junction where the stems met the core crystal. For there, at that strategic point, the MCQ3's builders had installed an anti-grav generator.

The MCQ3 floated effortlessly, kept station perfectly, defied the planet's relentless pull, all without the beat of so much as a single set of wings.

It made perfect sense, the ship was destined for planet-fall on unknown worlds. We obviously could not predict atmospheric makeup, pressures, up-drafts, and so on, in advance. It was entirely impractical to imagine a wing-supported crystal cruising the atmosphere of some unforeseen alien world. The anti-grav made perfect sense.

But the problem was, it made sense for our own home crystals as well. The anti-gravs were easy enough to build. If they were installed on the home

23

crystals it would free people up for things other than the main task of lifting. Life would be nothing but free flight!

As a gamer I found it fascinating. It was exactly a game scenario: Make a single, vital change in a society, and watch what happens. What would happen if we Ketrans were freed from this cooperative need to keep home afloat in the atmosphere? No one knew.

I gazed up at the MCQ3. There was no avoiding the emotions that accompanied that sight. I'd have sold my sire and dam into surface mining to go aboard. Deep worms, I wanted to go.

Wasn't happening. "What?" I mocked myself savagely. "No need for a game-playing adolescent aboard the greatest interplanetary expedition ever?"

Let it pass. Let it breeze on by, Toomin. Not on the past but on the future fix your range finder.

"That's right," I muttered darkly, "take refuge in platitudes."

I flapped wing and headed up. Not toward the MCQ3. No, not that way, but vectoring away from it, up toward the violet perches where I was to meet my friends to listen to the announcement. The last place I wanted to be in this frame of mind, but they, poor fools, still held out hope.

We had all applied to be accepted as nonessen-

24

tial crew. Why not? There's a natural affinity between gamers and planetary explorers. Or so we told ourselves.

I caught a lovely baffle breeze and soared effortlessly upward, up and up past all of Azure Level, up to Violet Level and the scooped-out hollow of the perches.

Redfar/Inidar was there waiting, zooming lazily with Escobat (whose game name was Wormer), and Doffnall, a rare female gamer, who used the game name Aguella.

"Hey, Ellimist," Aguella called out when she saw me. "I *memmed* that you managed to exterminate the Pangabans in record time."

Among ourselves we tended to use our game names. It was a silly affectation, another sign of the immaturity I was now able to see so clearly in all of us.

"I was playing a hunch," I said a little too gloomily to match her bantering tone. Then, trying to lighten the mood, I added, "I demand a rematch. Next time I'll manage to exterminate my side in even less time."

My friends laughed at that. We competed in the game, but there was also a sense that we four competed against the game, as though it was a common enemy we had to learn to subdue.

I recalled what Lackofa had said about the game

25

being necessarily limited. No doubt he was right. No doubt over time the patterns would become all too obvious and the game would thus become boring. But then, by that point, the game makers would have a new and improved game. They always did.

Wormer started talking about a scenario involving a three-way competition among a parasitic species, a predator species, and a symbiotic species. He was the only one who had played it so we listened closely. We quickly slipped into game speak as we free flew around the perches, checking out others of interest and being checked out in return. The violet perches were a great hangout for free-flying youths.

No one brought up the announcement, not at first anyway. No one wanted to seem unduly interested. We were breezy. Way too breezy to be obsessed over some slim chance at a true-life adventure. Anyway, we were gamers. The game was the thing.

And yet I noticed each of us in turn glancing at the pulpit where a Speaker would soon appear to deliver the news.

I wasn't nervous. I'd given up hope. There's nothing like a surrender to despair to settle your nerves. But the others were twitchy and it was hard not to catch a little of their turbulence.

I said, "You know, the truth is that underneath it all, the game has a set of assumptions. If we could codify these assumptions we could win every game." I was quoting Lackofa and passing it off as my own insight.

"Of course we could," Inidar said. "If. Very big 'if.' Huge 'if.' In fact it's so . . ."

He fell silent. He stared hard: *Four globes, no clouds, as the old saying goes.* Wormer and Aguella rotated and watched without even a pretense of disinterest.

What was I going to do? Pretend to fly away and tease some face-face with some strange female? I had to stay and wait. It was only polite.

I watched, waited along with them, as the Speaker drifted at a fuzzball's pace to the pulpit.

He was an oldster, his long quills more rust-red than clear. Speaker was a job for oldsters. They had the voices for it.

I didn't want to be nervous. I was. My entire brand-new edifice of indifference was washed away in an updraft of desire. Get it over with! Get it over with, oldster, and let me get on with my newly serious life.

"Here are the announcements," the Speaker said in a loud, carrying, professional voice.

"Violet and Pink Levels will begin cultivation of new spars. Each new spar will eventually grow eight yards, radial."

We didn't care. I didn't, anyway. Maybe Aguella or Wormer did, they're both Violets.

The Speaker went on. "There are seven days left before the Dance By of our own beloved home, with the Polar Orbit High Crystal. As most of you know, this is an event that takes place only once in every nineteen years. Free flights will be scheduled in half-intervals to allow the largest number of people to meet and mingle with our brothers and sisters of the Polar Orbit High."

I shrugged. Well, that was something different, at least. A change of routine. A chance to meet strangers and make cross-connections. I wasn't ready to propagate fortunately. So at least there'd be none of that pressure. None of us were old enough. Except maybe for Aguella.

I glanced at her, watching to see her reaction to the announcement. Was she blushing? What a strange thought to imagine Aguella becoming a dam. Disturbing somehow. She looked nothing at all like my dam. Far younger, for one thing. Prettier.

Aguella had a seriousness that Inidar and Wormer and I lacked. She had more than the game going on in her life. She was very into passive sensor theory.

In fact, one of her designs had been incorporated (in modified form) into the sensor array of the EmCee.

"Finally," the Speaker said portentously.

"Here it comes," Wormer muttered.

"I will announce the names of the nonessential crew chosen for the upcoming trip of the Mapping Crystal Quadrant Three. The names will be announced by level. From Pink Level: Pink Level, Seventy Spar, Yard One, Down-Messenger, Nine. Pink Level . . ."

"We could run a game before he gets to any of us," Inidar grumbled.

The moment of high drama was rather undercut by the realization that we had a long wait ahead of us. And yet, we did not budge. There was some desultory conversation, but with always an ear cocked.

And then, "Violet Level, Two Spar, Main Branch, Left-Messenger, One hundred twenty-nine."

Aguella gasped. For a long moment I had no idea why.

"Is that you?" I asked stupidly. I'm sure I'd known her formal name at some point but I'd long since forgotten it.

She nodded. She started to speak, then just nodded some more. She looked troubled more than elated. Almost worried.

I had no more time to be concerned with her strange reaction to good news. The Speaker had at long last reached Azure Level. Wormer sagged. Violet Level was done, and his name had not been called.

There were just seven names from Azure Level. My name was the fifth name spoken.

For a frozen moment of time my brain stopped synapsing. I stopped breathing. My wings faltered and I did a droop. "Did he say my name?" I whispered. "Forty-one, right? Not Thirty-one?"

Wormer did his best to be nice about it. He tried to breeze it. Maybe Inidar did his best, too, but his best wasn't great. He looked like a crasher, and I knew that anything I said to try and take away the hurt would just hurt him worse. Pity is never very comforting to the pitied.

But at some level their reactions were already irrelevant. I knew it, and so did they, sadly.

The four of us were now two and two. Wormer and Inidar would stay behind. Aguella and I would go.

chapter 4

I returned to my dock, barely making it in time. I clamped on and yelled up to Lackofa.

"Hey! Hey! Lackofa!"

He opened his eyes and favored me with his usual disapproving scowl. "What now?"

"I made it. I'm nonessential!"

"As nonessential as it is possible to be," he said dryly.

"Very funny, Lackofa, but you don't even have a faint chance of annoying me. Not today. I'm on the EmCee! We'll be crew together. I'm going!"

"Oh that. Yes, I know."

"How do you know? It can't be on the uninet yet. There's a mandated quarter-hour lag time for official announcements."

The uninet was a relatively recent development, barely a hundred years old, and no one wanted to obsolete the Speakers and their traditions.

Lackofa closed his eyes. I accessed the uninet. No, the announcement wasn't on yet. Wait, here it was, just coming up. I punched in and read my own name, my lovely, lovely name. I highlighted it in crimson letters and read it again.

A very fine name that looked very, very fine placed neatly near the bottom of the list. The sight of it filled me with profound satisfaction.

Then, I realized. "Hey, Lackofa. How did you know, if it's just now coming on the net?"

No answer.

"You did it," I accused. "You sponsored me!"

"Why would I do that?" he growled.

"Why would you do that?" I echoed with a different emphasis. "You don't even like me. I'm a gamer. A losing gamer. I'm a hundred and seventy-ninth in the rankings, out of nine hundred and nine registered gamers in my set. Why me?"

Lackofa didn't answer at first, but I guess he realized I wasn't going to let him off the hook. He sighed again, grumbled inaudibly to himself for a moment, then, sounding like a person who is being forced to confess to a crime, said, "I have developed a morbid curiosity about your failures, Toomin. I'm a biologist so I have access to your DNA map. You are in fact one hundred and ninety-fourth in the rankings — your loss earlier has bumped you fifteen slots."

"Ouch."

"But in terms of pure analytical intelligence you are very near the peak."

"I am?"

"Yes, and don't play coy with me. You know you're smarter than gamers who beat you regularly. You lose games you should win, not deliberately, but stubbornly. You're playing the game at a different level. Not trying to win, trying to win with kindness. Altruism."

I was embarrassed. Amazed that Lackofa had been paying attention to me at a level that I never suspected.

"Anyway," Lackofa said. "We have any number of brilliant scientists, brilliant analysts, brilliant communicators, brilliant theoreticians, brilliant physicists, brilliant techs, and brilliant astronomers on board the MCQ3. I asked myself what we didn't have, and the answer came to me: We had no brilliant losers. So, yes, I sponsored you. Now please shut up, I have work to do."

He closed his eyes and shut me out, this time for real.

Brilliant loser? Was it possible to be simultaneously flattered and insulted?

Evidently.

A *memm* popped up, an invitation to a game

from a gamer named Dryhad. I refused. This was not the time for a game. I had deep thoughts to think; plans to make; arrangements to arrange.

Didn't I? Yes, absolutely. It was definitely not time for a game. First and foremost, I had to learn everything there was to learn about MCQ3, about Zero-space engines, about Quadrant Three and its major star systems.

I accessed the data on MCQ3. The summary alone would take me a year to digest. No time for all that. Besides, I didn't need the technical stuff, I just needed . . . well, for now I just needed the pictures.

Yes, yes, there she was. A true deep-space ship. My deep-space ship. My own personal MCQ3, I loved her already.

Brilliant loser?

At least I wouldn't go aboard her unprepared, looking like some lost fool who couldn't tell inner from outer. I was going to memorize every square inch of her.

So little time. Nineteen days. So much to do and no time at all. Practically no time at all. Nineteen days!

Deep worms, it was going to seem like forever.

chapter 5

My mind was focused sharply, even obsessively, on the MCQ3 and its launch, but everyone else was more interested in the Dance By of Polar Orbit High. The Polars were Ketran, of course, just like us, but with a possibly different society. I say possibly because we only encountered them every nineteen years.

Naturally we had secondhand reports from the other crystals who'd encountered them and gone on to do a Dance By with us. Just last year we'd done the Dance with the Equatorial High Crystal Two, our sister crystal, and they'd had an encounter with Polar just three years before that.

Still, getting secondhand reports from three years before is not the way to understand a civilization. And in any case, some of what the Two's had told us about the Polars was a bit strange.

For one thing the Polars supposedly were very involved in quill coloring. Not of itself a bad thing, I guess, but weird. I mean, you have the quills you're born with, why would you want them to be green or whatever?

But more profound, the Polars were said to be making great strides in atmospheric communications. This, of course, would be a breakthrough of world-shattering proportions. If anyone could figure out how to punch a wave signal through the background radiation they'd be able to communicate crystal to crystal. We would no longer be a planet of thirty-two independent crystals; we'd have all thirty-two hooked up to a planetary uninet. I'd be able to play against gamers from entirely different crystals!

I'd be able to lose to people I might never actually see.

But maybe it was all just rumors. It's one thing firing electrons through a crystal, it's a very much harder thing to do it through the air.

The Dance By of the Polar Orbit High Crystal would not last long, only a few hours. Neither of us was willing to undergo the terrific exertions necessary to slow our momentum and then restart. So we'd have at best three hours where we could free fly across the divide. And individually we'd have far less.

I was scheduled early when the distance was greatest. I was young. You wouldn't expect the oldsters to want to free fly for half an hour only to have a ten-minute encounter.

The whole of society was excited. Me? Not so much. I had other things on my mind.

I was docked, gliding through a uninet sim of the MCQ3 for the twentieth time, when I heard a voice calling me from very close by. I opened my eyes and there was Aguella. She had come right to my spar.

"Ellimist. What are you doing?"

I blinked. "What?"

"It's time. What, are you ignoring time cues? It's time! The Dance By."

"Oh. Right." I released my docking talons and peered southward. Polar had been in sight for most of a day now, but it had grown quite a bit larger in the last few hours. In fact my first thought was that we were going to intersect.

Aguella was grinning expectantly, waiting for something. Waiting for me to notice something. I frowned and returned my attention to Polar. Then I yelled.

"Hey!"

Aguella nodded. "Yeah."

"They've gone asymmetrical. Look at that new growth." The sphere, or what should have been a sphere, had a definite lump. The lump was only a tenth of the diameter, but way too large to be simply new growth awaiting a trim.

"Not asymmetrical," Aguella said. "Or at least

that's not the end goal, I think. I may be wrong, but I suspect a pattern. You can't see it from here, but I think they're trying to flatten the sphere in all directions. I think this lump has a matching lump opposite."

"Why would they . . ."

"Airfoil," she said triumphantly. "The Polars are making an airfoil."

For the first time in seven days I completely forgot about MCQ3. An airfoil! It was something out of fiction. It was no surprise that a sphere was harder to keep lifted than an airfoil. The airfoil could fly into the prevailing breeze and actually derive lift.

It was the utopian's answer to engines. Attaching engines to a crystal might destroy social cohesion, but an airfoil design would still require the people to lift. They would just have to lift a lot less. I once read that an efficient airfoil design would allow for half the people to be in free flight at any given time.

"That would be so breezy if they did it," Aguella said jealously. "I wonder if we'll ever try."

"Maybe," I said doubtfully. I recalled to mind images of the Wise Ones in council. Half of them were so old they were more drag than lift. I was willing to bet some of them had dropped dead on the spot when they saw the Polar's airfoil.

"Come on, let's get going," she urged.

We Four-Effed: flew free, fast, and furious. Not a moment to be lost. Aguella, being female, was faster than me, of course, but she restrained her impatience to allow me to keep up. I rode her wind, staying just behind her. This had the advantage of offering me a view that included both the amazing soon-to-be airfoil and Aguella herself. She had lovely pods.

Not the point, Toomin, I thought. *Not really what you need to be thinking about right now.*

Mones! She was spreading the *mones* for me!

For me? No, surely not. Aguella could have any male she wanted. She was beautiful, well formed, sturdy, intelligent, funny, beautiful, very beautiful.

That was several too many "beautifuls," I said to myself. It was true then: Aguella was spreading *mones*. And I was helpless in her slipstream.

I cut left, clear of her backwash. It slowed me down a bit but that was good. Anything to bring me clear air.

I sucked fresh air but it was almost too late. My quills were ticklish for sure. How could she do this? She was a fellow gamer! It was an outrage, and with the trip coming up, and the Dance By and . . . it was a low trick, that was for sure.

She had to have noticed my sudden, graceless

exit. She had to know why I'd done it. Great, now she'd be angry at me, and I was so completely not in the frame of mind to be diplomatic and polite and play it breezy. My brain had crashed.

"Almost there," she said. "Look!"

"What? Look at what?" I yelped.

"There are the first Polars, just ahead. They look to be about our age."

"Yeah, well, we're not exactly the same age, you know, Aguella."

She laughed. It was a disturbing laugh. "We're almost the same age, Toomin — physically. Now, psychologically . . ." She laughed again, a mocking, condescending, yet frighteningly intimate laugh.

I gulped and tried not to read anything into the fact that she had used my chosen name, not my game name. She always called me Ellimist. Never Toomin.

Oh, this was great. Oh, this was just great.

I ignored her joke, her laughter, and, as well as I could, the lingering *mones.* I focused on the Polars.

There were two or three hundred of them in the air, spread around in an irregular two-mile space. Much as we Equatorials were. Like two sparkling clouds of veiner pests.

I looked back and saw my own home crystal. It looked very old-fashioned now, dull, compared with the radical Polar design that was now undeniably visible as an eventual airfoil. It made me a little defensive, I guess. Our home was larger, older, and I thought, more beautifully colored. But the Polar was the future, and that crunched.

I searched the Polars themselves, looking for the artificially colored quills I'd heard about, but they seemed no different than us. They each had "2 plus 4 equals 4 plus 2 and no one the better," as my pre-sire used to say: two pods, four wings, four eyes, and two arms.

Aguella and I picked out a pair of Polars who seemed willing to encounter us. They were about our age, both male. One had nice but natural yellow quills and ochre eyes. The other was more notable for his awkwardly large wings. We and they flew to intersection and floated at a polite distance.

"This is my friend Doffnall," I said, introducing Aguella by her chosen name. "I am Toomin."

"This is my friend Oxagast, and I am Menno," said the large-winged one.

"Well encountered," we all said simultaneously.

"You have a deep-space probe ready to launch!" Menno blurted.

He spoke at the very instant that I said, "You're configuring an airfoil!"

We all four laughed and I at least felt more com-

41

fortable. Their curiosity matched ours, and we had something to boast of after all.

"Yes, it's the Mapping Crystal Quadrant Three," I said, then, without even a pretense of modesty added, "Doffnal and I are crew."

"Essential crew?" Oxagast demanded.

Aguella laughed. "No, sorry, neither of us is a scientist. We're just a couple of gamers who got lucky."

We chatted about gaming and about the possibility of developing a crystal-to-crystal uninet.

Menno seemed about to say something, had his mouth open, then closed it and forced a smile. Oxagast's open gaze went opaque.

"That would be great," Oxagast said blandly.

Then Aguella brought up the airfoil design. "Didn't your Wise Ones resist the idea?" Aguella asked.

The two Polars exchanged a glance. "They did. So we took a vote."

"A what?"

"We voted. Each of us was allowed to decide our position, yes or no, then we added up the totals. The airfoil design was approved by sixty-one percent of the votes cast."

Aguella and I must have looked fairly shocked.

Menno smirked, nodding knowingly at our disturbed expressions. "We've made some changes in our society."

"Some changes? Why?"

Menno waved his hand toward his home. "Because it was necessary. We can't let the Wise Ones stop progress. Change is coming. Big changes. The people decide now. We're just two years away from completing the airfoil. Our lives will never be the same."

"No, I guess they won't be," I said. Was I upset or jealous or both? I was definitely disturbed. That much I knew.

Oxagast seemed less enthusiastic than his friend Menno. "The idea is that people will have so much more free time once the airfoil is operational, we'll make huge leaps forward. That's the idea, anyway."

"Of course we will," Menno said. "That MCQ3 of yours? No offense, but it will be a toy compared to what we will build. Polar Orbit High will lead the way, and others will follow. By the time you return from Three Quadrant, things will be very different."

"Different isn't always better," I muttered. I was thinking of the Pangabans.

But Menno shot back. "You're a gamer and you're afraid of change? What games do you Equatorials play? Any game worth playing is about control. With voting and with the other changes that are coming we stop being the playing pieces, moved here and there by the Wise Ones. We all become the Wise Ones. We become the players instead of the played."

"In any game scenario there's a balance between change and stability," I argued. "The game — at least the way we play it — is to make the slightest, most unobtrusive change — and achieve the desired result."

"Much the same with us," Oxagast agreed. "Only lately some gamers," he inclined his head toward Menno, "some gamers are looking to change the rules."

"We call ourselves Intruders," Menno said with a self-conscious laugh. "We're getting a little more radical. Why minimalism? Why marginal changes? Why not get inside the game, stick ourselves right into the action, and take over? See what I mean? Why should the gamer be invisible in the game? Intrude!"

I got a time cue. Time to head back. Too little time, and yet I was relieved.

"Well encountered," I said a little too hastily.

Aguella and Oxagast echoed the farewell. But Menno rudely met my gaze and said, "Don't be afraid of change, Equatorial. It's coming, whether you like it or not." Then, to my utter amazement, he clasped his hands together tightly and yelled the single word, "Intrude!" It wasn't a greeting or a farewell, it was a statement of belief. It was a challenge.

Aguella had said very little during the encounter, but on the way back she would scarcely shut up.

"He's right," she said. "Look what they've done! Airfoil. Why? They changed the rules, didn't they? Same thing in the game, they changed the rules."

"Yeah, well, he didn't exactly mention whether he won a lot of games," I pointed out.

"Maybe someday we'll be able to play against them," Aguella said.

"Maybe sooner than you think," I said, remembering the Polars' strange, constrained looks when I mentioned crystal-to-crystal communication.

Had the Polars solved that problem? That would be a true revolution, far more profound even than replacing the government of the Wise Ones.

Of course their transmission would be pretty pointless until other crystals had receivers. Otherwise they'd be a voice crying in the wind, unheard.

So I thought, and comforted myself with that illusion.

chapter 6

The next day, with the Polar Orbit High long gone from sight, I went aboard the MCQ3 for the first time.

There are sims and then there is reality. And let me say that no sim, no matter how good, matches reality. The problem with a sim is that you know it's a sim. Reality on the other hand, well, it's real.

Lackofa, as my sponsor, was my tour guide. Aguella had been chosen by the usual process, so she was sponsorless, and thus had both a disadvantage and an advantage.

The disadvantage was that she had no one to go to for answers. So she stayed hung with me, which was nice. The advantage she had was that she didn't have to worry about embarrassing her sponsor.

Lackofa's welcoming words to me were, "Just try not to be a complete idiot, okay? That's all I ask."

The MCQ3 was built along fairly standard lines. She was a single-hue cultivated crystal, ovoid rather than spherical. There was dockage for one hundred and four crew — essential and supernumerary. But of course no one provided lift. We could lift if that familiar motion made us feel more comfortable, but lift was irrelevant, unnecessary. A small taste, I suppose, of what an airfoil world would be like.

The MCQ3 existed within a force field that contained an atmosphere and would, we hoped, deflect most space debris. Should the force field ever fail we would lose our atmosphere. The backup system was a maze of pipes buried within the spars and masts that delivered breathable air to each dock.

"You simply pull the tube extension from the collar, thus," Lackofa demonstrated. "And you place it into your airhole, thus. Then breathe normally until the force field comes back up, or until you freeze to death, whichever comes first."

"What if we're not docked?" Aguella asked. "What if we're in one of the perches?"

"There are emergency accesses there," Lackofa said. "Good question. You're thinking ahead."

That made me open my eyes a bit. Was Lackofa looking for some face-face with Aguella? She wasn't *moning* again, was she? No, I would notice that.

I shook the sense memory out of my intakes and ruffled my wings to put it behind me. Didn't work. Other guys will warn you about being *moned;* what they don't talk about is how long the effect lasts.

"What if we're flying through Zero-space when the force field fails?" I asked.

Lackofa favored me with a withering glare. "We would drop instantly out of Z-space and appear back in normal space, where you would once again breathe through the tube or freeze to death. Oh, and by the way? It's hard to fly in a vacuum. So if we lose atmosphere you'll want to be docked."

I had a flash of myself beating my wings helplessly, futilely in space while the MCQ3 zoomed away toward some distant star.

Well, no one ever said space travel was safe. Generation 9561 claimed to have lost nearly ten percent of Generation 9547, the first Generationals to attempt space travel, and six percent of Generation 9548. Even as recently as 9558 they were losing substantial numbers in space-related accidents.

Then again, individual Generationals die pretty easily. It's kind of what they do. Corporate lifeforms just don't put up much of a fight over every interchangeable member.

"Follow me, stay close, don't touch anything," Lackofa instructed. He flew upward and we fell in place behind him. Up and up through byzantine, unfamiliar spars, past dockages, some that were still being installed and polished.

He led us to a perch like nothing I'd ever seen before — not even in the sim. It was a tipped bowl perhaps fifty feet across, all filled with blinking lights, readouts, and video displays. All of it constructed of metals and carbon filament and flat-crys. It was faintly claustrophobic, all that opaqueness wrapped around you.

"What is this?" I wondered. "It's not in the sim!"

"No," Lackofa said. "This is the backup command center. In case of catastrophic damage to the core crystal, these machines can be used to continue flying the vessel."

"How?"

"This unit is self-contained. You can't see it but it has its own engines, generates its own force field. In the case of catastrophic damage to the crystal itself, this pod can detach, break free, and keep flying."

"Without . . . without most of the crew," I said, unwilling to believe anything so monstrous. "And it's not in the sims."

Lackofa's eyes were hard. "No, it's not in the sims. And it won't be on the uninet at all. You need to understand something: This isn't your old life. This trip is a little more than an innocent scientific excursion. And it's definitely not a game."

His tone sent a shiver through me. Aguella and I exchanged significant looks.

We were keeping station outside the hard-edged, darkened perch. Floating far above our home crystal, well within home air. But all of a sudden I knew we had crossed over a boundary.

"What's out there?" I asked Lackofa.

He shook his head slowly. "We don't know for sure. But two years ago a vessel of unknown origin popped out of Z-space just a million miles from us and lit up our orbital sensors. The drop-pods are released only once every six months as you know, to prolong the life of the sensors. But by good luck we discovered the ship just two months after it emerged. We sent a drone out to intercept and survey. The drone never returned. Two months later we got the answer from another sensor's drop-pod. The alien vessel had fired on our drone and destroyed it using some sort of high-energy beam weapon. There were no life signs aboard the ship. It had been programmed to defend itself, I suppose. We modified a drone with a defensive force field and faster engine and sent it back to intercept the alien vessel again.

"This time we got lucky. The alien craft fired at the drone but before it could adjust to the defensive system, the drone had glue-docked to the alien vessel and was draining its computer of data.

"Just one problem: As the drone detached for reentry, the vessel fired again and damaged the drone. We recovered it but were only able to save a part of the data."

"How much do we know?" Aguella demanded.

Lackofa hesitated. Then, "You two understand this clearly, I hope: None of this ever becomes known to the people at large. I mean that on penalty of closure." He repeated it slowly, deliberately. "On penalty of closure."

That rocked me. Closure? For revealing a secret? They would undock me? Cut me off to free fly till I died of starvation and loneliness and finally augered into the lava fields below?

"Every alien race we've encountered has been benign," Lackofa said. "But this race, the race that built this ghost ship, was not. The evidence is that they respond with extreme violence to even the slightest provocation. Extreme violence. They call themselves Capasins. Since the ship emerged from the direction of Quadrant Three, we assume the Capasin planet is there. The mission of the MCQ3 is to contact this race and attempt to reach terms of peace."

"What if these Capasins are not interested in peace?" Aguella asked.

Lackofa smirked. "Then we'll hope to get home with enough information to allow us to meet the challenge. One thing we know: The Capasins don't know we exist. If we meet them we will keep our location strictly secret. Sometimes," he added thoughtfully, "the things that seem to be problems are actually blessings in disguise."

"What are you talking about?"

"Generation 9561's home planet has such low background radiation that they communicate regularly through transmission and reception of radio waves. Those waves propagate, you know." He waved his hand vaguely skyward. "Generational waves spreading endlessly through space. Who knows who will receive and perhaps comprehend those transmissions? Who knows what attention the Generationals may already have attracted. We, on the other hand, remain invisible to the galaxy. Maybe not such a bad thing."

chapter 7

Within three weeks I knew the actual MCQ3 as well as I knew the sim. I knew every mast, every spar, every perch, every backup system. I even knew the engines, as well as anyone can know a Z-space engine.

I had met many more crew members, essential and non. I'd even been introduced to one of the three Wise Ones who would be commanding. He was a grim oldster who managed to grunt indifferently at me before going back to his work.

I spent every free flight on the vessel. And my free-flight time had been tripled. (We were days away from launch and I'd already been discounted as a lift factor.)

I had very little time for gaming and I'm afraid that Inidar resented that. Our old relationship was strained now. Not just because I couldn't play, but because of why I couldn't play.

We kept exchanging *memms,* talking about scheduling games, but they never happened.

Instead, I saw a lot of Aguella. I kept waiting for

53

her to *mone* me again, but to my great relief it never happened. Very relieved.

Although I kind of wondered why she didn't. Had I done something wrong? Was it the way I'd reacted? Basically like a panicky juvie?

Didn't matter. There was no place for that kind of thing on a vital and dangerous deep-space mission.

Just would have liked to know why, that's all. And I got a hint as the two of us were assisting in the installation of the last few docks.

It was the two of us, and a female with the chosen name of Jicklet. Jicklet was essential crew — fifth technician. She knew what she was doing but unlike lots of people who are experts, she wasn't impatient with our relative stupidity.

"It's the whole point of nonessential crew," she explained, tightening a collar down till the adhesive oozed. "You're here to learn a little of everything. That way we'll always have backup. Okay, now you, Toomik, use the scrape-saw to slice off the excess glue."

"It's Toomin."

"Yeah, whatever you say, Toomid. Careful. Leave a bead."

I sliced the already half-dry adhesive, carefully

leaving an eighth-inch bead. I was less successful at cupping the curling excess into the slop pit.

"You have to be careful not to drop any," Jicklet said. "We're right above the engines. You don't want to be down there in an en-suit burning it off the pods. There you go. Good work. Now polish it down and give me a yell when you're ready for me to look it over."

She beat wing and elevated to the other pair of amateurs she was supervising. Aguella and I shared a sigh of relief that she was gone.

And then Equatorial High Crystal blew apart.

A hammer blow on my head. Wings snapped back by the concussion. Spinning. Fire, fire everywhere!

One second I was working and grinning at Aguella, and in the next instant my ears were bleeding, my eyes swimming. My mind was a mess of shattered bits and pieces.

What was happening?

I was cut in a dozen places by flying shards. A six-inch spike of crystal was lodged in my left pod. I pulled it out, yelling and crying and falling through the air as I did so.

What was happening?

Aguella — where was she? Nothing I saw made

sense. Debris still flying all around me, falling away now, but twirling and glittering as it fell.

The MCQ3 still held station. Where was Aguella?

"Aguella! Aguella!"

I heard a moan, barely audible past the ringing in my ears. I looked up and saw her. She was using her talons to cling to an unpolished bit of spar.

And then it happened again. And this time I saw it. I looked up at my friend, at the streams of dull, burnt-orange blood coming from her face. But past her, above the MCQ3, up through the masts and spars I saw the raked cylinders, the arched neck, the dagger points of an alien ship. It cruised slowly through the atmosphere, taking its time. Nothing like a Generational or Illaman ship. Nothing like anything I'd seen or imagined.

It seemed to circle slowly around my home crystal, watching, waiting, and then it fired again. A beam of energy, pale red. The beam lanced down into the core of my home crystal, my poor damaged home. This time I expected the concussion as overheated crystal exploded, blew apart.

My world dropped, fell away. It was in two pieces now. A fragment equal to a third of the whole spun, spiraled down. Wings beat frantically but the balance was lost. And too many wings would never beat again.

The remnant of Equatorial High Crystal was scarred and burned. Ends broken off. Jagged and rough. But it still maintained lift. I could see thousands of my brothers and sisters, all straining, all lifting together. Free flyers were rushing to dock anywhere they could, anywhere to provide lift.

But the alien ship wasn't done with its work. This time no beam weapon. This time it sprayed a cloud of flechettes. Small, so small they could barely be seen with the naked eye, millions of tiny shredding metal hooks. The sound was like a volcano blowing. The flechettes sprayed for five seconds, no more, but at the end of that time every unshielded Ketran was torn apart. The entire crystal might have been dipped in blood.

The bodies began to fall away. The crystal itself began to fall. Straight down, down, and gathering speed, with no one left to hold it up any longer.

It would take a long time to fall three hundred miles.

chapter 8

"Aguella!" I flapped to her. She was conscious, but barely.

"Dock you fools! Dock now!" a voice yelled. Jicklet. "We're powering up!"

I heard the low whine of the engines warming. I grabbed Aguella as well as I could; her wings were beating but weakly. I grabbed her and steered her, hauled her to the nearest dock. The dock we'd just finished installing. I pressed her back against it.

"Clamp on! Listen to me: Clamp on!"

She nodded, eyes wild, wandering. I saw her chest tighten. She was docked. Now it was my turn. The nearest open dock was fifty feet away.

The alien had spotted us. At first we must have looked like a part of the home crystal. But now he could see that we were still flying, that we were self-contained. And yet he was in no hurry. Why should he be? We'd been unable to resist. We were helpless.

The alien ship drifted lazily around, bringing its dagger tip to bear on us. With numb fingers I fumbled to the dock, twisted, lined up, and the alien fired.

The beam this time. Deadly accurate. It hit us on center.

But the force field had been raised by someone thinking more clearly than I. The red beam glowed and a disc of bright light appeared at the limits of the force field.

The alien sheered off. I was on the ship's uninet now, hooked in, able to watch the readouts from the engines. At ninety-five percent of power they could be engaged. We were at sixty-five percent.

Everyone I knew was dead. My sire and dam, dead. Inidar was dead. Wormer, dead. I looked down and saw her, my home, a bright glint still falling away. How long to fall three hundred miles? How long till it hit the lava fields, crumpled, and was burned out of existence?

The alien ship hovered close. It seemed curious. Interested. Like a scientist studying some new microbe under a lens.

Then a small craft, a boxier, winged version of the main ship, dropped from its belly. It hovered then flew close, probing toward us, feeling for the force field. It stopped. Engine readout at eighty percent.

The small craft nosed forward, very slowly. It pressed against the force field, pushed at it. The field held. Engines at eighty-four percent. I could see a single shape, a form through a transparent window at the front of the little ship. He was no more than twenty yards away. I could see him, he could see me. It had become intimate now, personal.

The small craft began to glow, as if it were heated from the inside. It glowed brighter and brighter till the light hurt my eyes.

"It's going to get through," I said.

We had nothing. No weapons. I understood weapons in the abstract, what gamer doesn't? Besides, we knew that Generational ships were always lightly armed. But we ourselves had none. Never had.

The nose of the ship pushed through the force field. It was slow going. It was absorbing and deflecting the force field and it was slow going, but it was faster than the rising blue bar and numbers of the engine readout. It would be in before we could escape. Once a hole was opened, the cloud of flechettes.

Nothing. No weapon. Hand tools. The scrapers and scorers I'd been using for . . .

Scoring. Score and break!

It was absurd. A losing move. The kind of stupid move that would leave other gamers gasping with laughter.

The only move I had.

I undocked. I flew to a naked spar point. It was sharp, undulled by the usual safety knob. How much weight could I carry? I should know how much a section of spar end would weigh, I should know, but I didn't, and no time now.

I guessed. Six feet. I could carry that much. I hovered by the spar end and fumbled, nearly dropped my scoring knife. I began to cut a ring around the foot-thick crystal. Cut. Cut. Don't worry about retaining the splinters now.

The score came full around. I flitted back and launched straight into the spar. It broke clean. Clean enough. Not a professional cut, but it would do.

I wrapped my arms around it and took the weight. Not so much weight, I could lift it. But it was awkward, hard to turn around.

I tucked it under my arm on one side, got a slight supporting purchase with one talon, and beat wing.

I flew straight for the small craft. Faster, fast as I could fly, reckless, no time to worry about it now, no time to wonder how I would survive impact.

As if in slow motion the face in the window turned. It had only two eyes, both forward-looking. Blue. Almost pretty. The blue eyes watched me, and then widened. What alien emotion? Fear? Derision? Amazement?

The light was blinding, barely could keep my eyes open, nothing but those blue eyes staring.

I struck. The point of the spar sliced into sheet metal, penetrated a foot, then stopped. I yanked it back. It came free.

I dropped, took the full weight, and this time stabbed upward directly beneath the alien crewman. Again the spear point stopped hard.

But now the glow was dying away. The electric buzz of energy fields was weakening.

Height, you fool, use gravity, a voice in my head shrieked. Of course!

I beat wing to gain altitude. Up, up, the blue eyes followed me, still, it seemed to me, more curious than malevolent.

Up twenty feet. Now! I plunged. My wings hammered the air and I dropped, spear point down.

The spear struck the alien craft just above the cockpit. The crystal penetrated. There was no explosion. Nothing dramatic. But as I released the spar and let momentum carry me down past the window, I saw that the alien was staring with no expression at all.

The spar point had penetrated the cockpit, and penetrated his large head.

At that moment, with the alien ship half in and

half out of the MCQ3's force field, our engines at last kicked in.

For a giddy, terrifying moment the entire universe collapsed around me. And a moment later I was floating without sensation of speed through the blank white nothingness of Zero-space.

The alien small craft was with us still. The alien I had destroyed still stared with beautiful blue eyes.

chapter 9

We emerged almost immediately from Zero-space. Only one of the vessel's Wise Ones had been aboard at the time of the attack. He appeared via uninet. I had met him very briefly. His current chosen name was Farsight. It was a name appropriate to his role. A Wise One's name.

"It is clear that Ket is under attack from an alien species of unknown origin. We are calculating a return trajectory and hope to place this vessel at the disposal of some other home crystal. Perhaps we can be of some assistance, though without weapons . . ."

Farsight's quills drooped and he lowered his eyes. He was very old. I hoped he was very wise. I wanted to believe he was. But he seemed unaware of the fact that we had an alien craft in tow.

Nonessential crew did not *memm* a Wise One. It wasn't done. Especially not in the midst of a crisis. But I was too jangled to be very concerned with social niceties.

I keyed up a waiting *memm*. He could ignore it if he chose.

I was gratified (and encouraged) to see that Farsight responded by immediately opening a channel. His head jerked up and he seemed to be staring right at me.

"It's still with us?"

"Yes, Wise One," I replied. "It's trapped within our force field. Or half in and half out."

It was not encouraging to realize that the people in charge had no real idea what had happened down here by engine three. Had no idea that the force field had been compromised. The MCQ3 had been caught more unprepared than I'd imagined.

I *memmed* a very brief description of what had happened.

The reaction was immediate. There was a flurry of wings and half a dozen people zoomed past me, vectoring toward the alien ship. Lackofa was one of them.

He paused and yelled, "Well, come on, hero. You killed him."

It was a typical backhanded slap/stroke from Lackofa. But it stung more than it soothed. I had killed. It was the second of the Five Laws: Take no sentient life. Second in importance only to: Lift for all.

I glanced back at Aguella. She was alive. But in no condition to join me. A long period of dockage, that's what she needed. She'd be fine. She'd be fine.

Had to be fine. Her survival had become vital to me. She had to live. No one else had.

I undocked and flew to catch up with Lackofa. Jicklet was with him. Seven of us flitted before the nose of the craft, nervous, jumpy, unsure of how to proceed.

"It's a container," someone said. "Everything that matters will be within. We need to get inside."

Of course the word "inside" filled us each with dread, though we had surely just survived worse than mere enclosure.

"The sheet metal's pretty thin," Jicklet said. "If it wasn't then the spar tip wouldn't have penetrated. But see? There are wires and other sorts of primitive conduit running through the skin. I can peel the metal easily enough. The wiring will take a bit longer if we're to save what's here. And if you want me to open the hatch, well, I'd first have to trace each wire."

She waited for an answer. For orders. It occurred to me that no one had any clear sense of who, if anyone, was in charge.

Finally Lackofa said, "Preserve the function of the alien ship. But hurry. Get us an opening."

Jicklet went to work, and two of the others zipped in to help her. They were experienced techs,

Lackofa and I and the remaining members of our strange rescue party were not.

Lackofa looked more worried than I've ever seen him. Me I didn't need any help feeling grim. The memory of my home falling away trailing a mist of Ketran blood behind it was still fresh. Would always be.

I could see the alien too well now. His lidless eyes were darkening. As if some deeper blue pigment were seeping into the iris. His head was bulbous, large by our standards. He had no wings. He had a beak for a mouth, a sharp, downturned thing that gave him a sad, disappointed expression. A number of long, thin, multiple-jointed arms hung limp. His skin was a green so dark it might almost have been black. The long crystal spear entered his head from directly above.

"Capasin," Lackofa said in answer to my unspoken query. "I guess our mission of peace is canceled."

"What do we do now?" I asked.

"You tell me, gamer."

Jicklet wiped her face. A nicked conduit had sprayed her with some pressurized fluid. She had closed it up. "That's as much as we can do. There are main structural supports back of this. If we cut those we'll never get her closed up again."

There was a squarish hole, lined with sharp curls of steel and jumbled wiring. A hole big enough for one of us to enter through — once the spar had been removed.

"Let's pull the spar out," Lackofa said quietly.

It was gruesome work. When we lifted the spear stuck and the alien corpse began to rise through the hole. Lackofa and one of the techs put their pods against the alien's soft, yielding skull, and we pulled all at once. There was a sucking sound and the spear came away. The body fell in a heap on the deck of his ship.

Two of the techs flew the spar away for disposal. No one was going to suggest reattaching it. Not a killing weapon. No one looked at me. No one said anything, but no one looked at me, either.

"We need to see whether we can fly this thing," Lackofa said. He licked his lips. He wasn't volunteering. Neither was Jicklet.

It wasn't hard to understand: An enclosed space was bad enough. An enclosed space occupied by a corpse was still worse. Dead bodies were not meant to be kept around. They fell away from their docks to burn up on the surface below. Anything else was hideous and perverted.

And yet I had a relationship with this dead alien. He was mine in some indefinable way.

"I'll do it," I whispered.

"You don't have to," Lackofa said kindly. But his eyes said different: If not you, gamer, then who?

"You'll have to help hand me in and out," I said. I looked pleadingly at Lackofa and Jicklet. "You'll get me out?"

Jicklet put her hand on my arm. "If I have to slice the ship up like a fresh bat, we'll get you out."

I took a couple of deep breaths. No time to waste. Farsight would be anxiously waiting our report. He wanted — we all wanted — to get back to Ket.

"Look for weaponry," Lackofa said.

I nodded. I'd look for weaponry. If I could fight down my urge to panic and lacerate my wings in an enclosure rage.

I landed on the ship. I folded my wings tightly. *Do it in one quick drop, Toomin. All at once.*

I stepped off, fell through the hole, and landed with one pod on blood-slicked floor and the other on a pair of the alien's arms.

I fell over, prostrate on the deck, my face inches from the Capasin's now-opaque eyes. The scream was in my throat before I could think.

I screamed, panic, all around me, closed in! No sky! No sky!

"Close your eyes!" Lackofa yelled. "Toomin, shut your eyes. Don't look!"

69

His own fear-edged voice scared me more. But I closed my eyes. Squeezed them shut. And my wings stayed tight.

I breathed hard, then softer, forcing myself to be calm, calm.

Slowly open one eye, Toomin. No, look away from the Capasin. Up. Look up at the hole, look up at the open hole and beyond at the star field. A night sky. Not my night sky, but a sky just the same.

Sky. Okay, I can do this. I can.

I opened my other eyes. I climbed erect, shaky, but not panicky. But it took real effort to tear my longing gaze away from the safe square above me, to look away from the sky and the faces of my companions.

The cockpit of the ship was small by any standard. And it was made smaller still by the instrumentation that seemed at first to be a randomly assembled pile of black boxes with glowing green lights.

It reminded me of nothing so much as our own emergency backup systems. Primitive systems made of metals, using electrons rather than photons to carry data. And all designed to be manipulated by touch rather than *memm*.

It was crude. How could it be so crude? The larger version of this ship had murdered my home

70

crystal in less than five minutes. How could this ship be so laughably backward? It was an insult, an outrage.

"You need to hurry, Toomin."

"Yes."

"Are you okay?"

"Yes. Yes. I just . . . it's not right. I mean, they're . . . Why would they . . ."

"Toomin, this isn't the time."

"They killed everyone!"

"I know, Toomin. But we don't have time right now. Don't think about that. Focus. It's . . . it's a game, Toomin. It's a game and you're Ellimist. Analyze. Don't feel, it's just a game."

Yes. That's what it was. A sim, not real. There had been no dagger-sharp ship. No pale red beam. No tornado of flechettes. A game. A problem.

I shook myself, loosened my painfully tight-gripped wings. There were controls. Physical fly-by-wire controls. Some would run the ship. Some would be for simple maintenance and environmental functions. Then there would be the weapons.

What could that symbol mean? Was it ship's attitude? Probably. At least to my own Ketran sensibilities. Yaw. Roll. Attitude. Air speed? And beside those . . . yes, yes, those had to be flight controls. Thrust. Reverse thrust. Microthrusters.

Okay, then those long things, those jointed sticks, those were the weapons controls. It would require skill to fly and fight the ship simultaneously. Could I at least fly it?

Not well. But yes. Maybe. Maybe as well as a flightless alien, anyway. What did a surface creature understand of flight after all?

"Ellimist?" Lackofa prodded gently but insistently.

I took a deep breath. My next words would seal my fate, perhaps all our fates. "You can report to Farsight I can bring this ship within our field. And fly her when we get home."

"It has weapons?"

"Yes. I don't know what they do. But yes."

"They kill, that's what they do," Lackofa said grimly. "And it may be that's what we need."

chapter 10

I was not in touch. No *memms*. And no time for instructions beyond those passed on from Lackofa. He shuttled to dock, quickly explained what we'd learned to Farsight, then raced back to instruct me.

"We're jumping back through Z-space. We think from this short distance we can hit reentry pretty accurately. The Wise One's orders are that you and I take control of this alien vessel and carry out any defensive actions possible."

"You and I? You mean . . . you understand we'd have to be sealed in."

"Yes," Lackofa said flatly. "Yes. Jicklet will seal us in."

I felt sick at the thought. But not as sick as Lackofa. He was oozing *mones*. Fear. The smell of it triggered my own panic reflex and I had to struggle to maintain my shaky control.

The Illamans travel for years at a time locked in their rectangular spacecraft. But Illamans are surface dwellers, used to taking shelter in constructions. For a Ketran the very idea of being enclosed is horrible.

Jicklet grabbed Lackofa's arm. "Can you do this?

I'll take your place. You're a biologist, I'm a tech. It's not a job for a biologist."

Lackofa looked for one drawn-out moment like he might grab at the safety hammock she was offering. But he shook his head no, unable to speak, but signaling no, he would do this himself. He would endure what no Ketran could endure.

"Like you told me, Lackofa, close your eyes," I said to him. "Close your eyes. I'll help you down."

He had nothing to say, no wisecrack or wry observation. He was beyond that. And now I found that helping him with his fear helped me with my own.

I lowered him down gently to stand beside me. He was as stiff as a length of conduit.

I kept talking to him, reassuring him as Jicklet and her fellows worked to seal us in. No sky. No sky at all. *Just keep talking to Lackofa,* I told myself, *just keep talking, don't want him to panic, no panic, no panic.*

I realized my own eyes were squeezed shut. I opened them a slit and looked out through the window. What kind of sub-Ketran beast could tolerate this? Peering at the sky through a false transparency? Locked inside a steel box? The Capasins must be animals. No sentient could live like this.

Not fair, not accurate, of course; both the Illamans and the Generationals endured captivity and were sentient. But I wasn't in the mood to be reasonable. I wasn't in the mood to do anything but scream.

"Are you okay?" Lackofa asked me. He had pried open one eye.

"No, are you?"

"No."

"Come on. I'll show you what I've figured out."

"Do we have a name for this death crate?"

"Crate. That's good enough," I muttered. I considered which control stick would be easiest for Lackofa to manage. "Here. Put one hand here. This controls thrust. Forward is more, back is less, twist left I think means reverse thrust."

He nodded. His quills were slowly draining their pink and the stench of terror *mones* was fading. He was scared but no longer near panic.

Through the window I saw the sky turn white. We had reentered Zero-space. In a few short minutes . . .

Lackofa looked away from the controls and down to the dead alien. "I was right. Probably Capasin," he said. Then he actually touched the head, turned it to one side, peered at it thoughtfully, and drew out a small instrument pouch. He was a biologist — an exobiologist, for that matter. I guess touching dead aliens was easy for him. Probably even comforting.

75

All at once the white sky was black again, black and star-filled. I could not see Ket. Had the navigator failed? Did we even have a navigator aboard? I was ready to ask Lackofa, when we rotated and all at once my home world rose into view, huge, close. The familiar red rivers and gray-green morasses, the brown-scarred deserts and puffy, pale green clouds, all lovely beyond enduring. It was a stab to the heart.

My world had been assaulted. I let the rage flow freely. It drove out the fear, a little at least.

The MCQ3 swooped down and down, into the edge of atmosphere. The force field glowed red as we slowed to atmospheric speeds. We were returning to our old station, looking for the home we all knew was gone.

Nothing. The sky was empty. The sky that should have been filled with the Equatorial High Crystal and all the tens of thousands of beating wings and happy faces and . . . all of it gone, leaving a soul-hollowing emptiness in the sky.

The ship turned away, reluctantly it seemed to me, though of course a crystal, even the EmCee, has no life, no emotion.

We raced along at supersonic speeds toward an intercept with our sister, Equatorial High Crystal

Two. We slowed in anticipation and found nothing but empty sky.

Another vector, another slow realization that where a thriving crystal should be was nothing but empty sky.

Around the planet. Station after station. Orbit after orbit. Race, then slow. Search an empty sky. Accept the unacceptable with mounting horror.

Twelve crystals gone. How many lives lost? Was anyone alive? Was anyone left alive anywhere?

We hit a cloud bank, a three-day bank where our recent dance partner, Polar Orbit High Crystal, should be. Maybe the cloud bank had hidden them, saved them.

We eased our way forward. I knew every eye was straining, searching. Surely if they knew of the alien attack the Polars would kill momentum and stay within the cloud.

We emerged into an oasis of sky. One of those wonderful clear holes that the bigger cloud banks sometimes develop. Polar Orbit High was there. It was moving as fast as it could, every wing beating, racing to cross the oasis and find shelter in the far towering cliff of clouds. But the airfoil was more a concept than a reality, and the Polars moved no faster than any crystal could.

The Capasin ship was two hundred yards above. Watching. Waiting.

"Why don't they attack?" I demanded. "Why do they wait?"

"Some creatures enjoy the hunt," Lackofa said with professional dispassion. "Some take pleasure from the kill."

Just do your slaughter, I raged impotently. Was it funny to them? Were the filthy aliens laughing as they watched the frail-winged creatures trying to move their home away at a fuzzball's pace?

Suddenly the Crate's sensors came alive. Farsight had lowered the force field and the Crate's sensors, liberated, were picking up data from the surrounding environment.

It was our signal. Our signal to . . . to do what, exactly?

I swallowed stale air and said, "Lackofa. Thrust."

"What?"

"Thrust. Fifty percent."

The result nearly crumpled us both. The Crate kicked forward. The dead alien rolled onto his belly. We blew away from the EmCee and shot toward Polar Orbit High Crystal.

My turn. I worked the controls with my two hands and very quickly discovered that my guesses about their function had been wrong. We arced downward at an airspeed just below supersonic.

"Pull up!"

"I know!" I yelled.

I twisted the stick and with a death shudder the Crate bottomed out, took the gees, and blew skyward again. I trimmed and we were aimed for the Capasin ship, still going way too fast.

No. I was thinking like a Ketran, not a Capasin. Engines not wings. A box not a body. More speed, not less.

"Increase to seventy-percent thrust."

"Are you crazy?"

"DO IT!"

Faster! Up and up and was I right about the weapons controls? Was I going to annihilate my own ship or, worse yet, hit the poor, fleeing Polars?

I squeezed a finger around a protruding ring.

The beam drew a perfect line through the air and hit the Capasin ship. There was a small explosion on the steel surface twenty feet back from the dagger's point.

I twisted and bellied the Crate out to zoom along the spine of the Capasin ship.

A shameful part of my mind thought, *Now, this is a game!*

chapter 11

It was a game. Like nothing I'd ever played. But it helped to think of it as a game. *Don't think of it as lives, actual lives. It's only a game. When it's all over Inidar and I will laugh and . . .*

Only Inidar was dead, wasn't he? And everyone . . . everyone.

I took my momentum and held it through a turn, making unchecked leeway that carried me a mile before I could engage thrust again. The leeway was a surprise. Not like winged flight.

I zoomed back, but the Capasin ship wasn't going to give me another free move. It was turning to meet us. Its much more powerful beam would soon be trained on us.

And yet, in this game perhaps the edge went to the smaller target? No way to know. I was guessing. Intuiting. Large, slow ship with powerful beam versus small, more maneuverable ship with a stinger. Who wins that game?

I fired. Missed!

"Take your time, aim carefully," I said.

"Do what?" Lackofa cried, hands clutching, blue-knuckled at the controls.

"Reverse thrust! Now!"

The alien body slammed into the back of my pods. But I kept my eyes on the window and saw the pale beam lance harmlessly by. I had made them miss!

Okay, then. That was the game. If my edge was maneuverability, I'd better maneuver.

The Capasins were surface dwellers, had to be. They flew their ships like surface dwellers, more in two dimensions than three.

"Up thrust. Twist it right and . . . yeah, like that!"

The Crate moved straight up, breaking free of the Capasin ship's plane. I tilted the nose of the Crate down and fired. A hit!

An engine. I'd hit an engine. Sizzling sparks and burning gases blowtorched from the hole. The engine pod blew apart. The Capasin ship spun, wild, out of control.

"They're disabled!" Lackofa cried triumphantly

I fired again. Not thinking. Not intellectualizing the decision, just knowing. I fired and the beam missed.

"What are you doing? She's disabled," Lackofa said.

Careful aim this time. I fired and held the ring down. The Capasin ship blew apart, a thousand small fragments.

"*Now* she's disabled," I whispered.

I glanced and saw Lackofa's horrified stare. I couldn't share it. It wasn't coldness on my part, I just knew the game and he didn't. The Capasins could have fired again and killed us. They could have fired flechettes at the crystal.

"The only win is a kill," I said. "That's the game. It's their game. They didn't disable the home crystal, they annihilated it. Their game, their rules."

Lackofa made no answer. We returned to the MCQ3 and parked the Crate within a flutter of the main perch. We had to confer with Farsight. I suggested Lackofa go.

"No. No, Ellimist, you. If I get out of this box I'll never get back in. I can rest here, keep my eyes closed. Or maybe look at this alien. You go. Besides, you're the gamer."

I didn't argue. He was right. He could be of some use examining the Capasin. I found the hatch and the release. Sky! I moved with deliberate slowness to exit the death trap. If I allowed myself to feel panic then like Lackofa, I'd never come back.

Once outside I saw that the Polars had killed momentum and were nearly stopped. They were maintaining station and half a dozen of their people were racing toward the EmCee. I beat wing and reached the main perch minutes ahead of them. Farsight would want my report first before having to cope with the no-doubt-panicked Polars.

The Wise One was resting in a hammock. He looked a bit orange. Sick or just old? Either way it was disturbing to see our only leader being supported in a hammock with never a stir from his tired wings. He was surrounded by advisers, maybe a dozen, all looking scared or confused or sly.

An officious female Pink I'd never met cut me off. "Go away. Farsight is busy."

"I am Azure Level, Seven Spar, Extension —"

"There is no Azure Level. Not anymore," she snapped. "Go away. Don't you know what's going on?"

"I'm the one who just blew up the Capasin ship," I said, not in any mood to have some mid-level pull rank on me.

Her eyes narrowed. Her expression went from stony dismissal to clever anticipation. "You're Toomin?"

Lackofa must have given them my chosen name. She grabbed me and nearly shoved me through the press of hovering advisers. All at once I was eyes-to-eyes with Farsight. I tried not to look at the hammock netting.

The Pink, whose name was Tatchilla, introduced me in quick, almost brutal terms. And she stayed close. I had the feeling I had just become her protégé. Even her property. Deep worms, were there really people who could think of ambition at a time like this?

Farsight fixed his gloomy eyes on me. "What do you know?"

An admirably appropriate question. "Lackofa believes they are Capasin. We can fly the Crate — the small ship of theirs — and we can fight her. But if we encounter more of their ships the odds do not favor Lackofa and me."

"More ships?" Tatchilla shrilled. "What do you mean more ships? Why should there be more ships?"

I was unsure. I was operating on instinct. I knew there were more ships, I knew it. But could I convince them?

"They play . . . I mean that they fight slowly. They take their time. They enjoy the process." I was on the verge of explaining that they were very much like a species called Endrids from the game. The Endrids, too, derived pleasure from the act of killing prey. But bringing the game into this would not help my credibility.

"The number of home crystals that are missing, presumed destroyed, the leisurely way the Capasins play . . . I assumed there are several more ships," I said, sounding unconvincing even to myself.

This was not good news. Tatchilla denounced the idea. She was no longer standing beside me claiming me as her own. "The issue is not this juvie gamer's fantasies, the issue is where we should take the EmCee. We need to find a new home crystal and claim protected status."

Just then the Polars arrived in a rush of wings and breathless questions.

"What is happening? That alien ship chased us as though preparing to attack!"

Farsight held up one feeble hand to cut them off. "Who speaks for you?"

"I am called Jardbrass," one of them said. "I will speak. This ship is within our rightful station. This is no Dance By. You are welcome here, but you will submit to our democratic authority."

"What?" someone guffawed. "We just saved your lives and you want to assert the primacy of your experimental system?"

"Saved our lives? We have no proof that the alien ship was —"

"You were running away," Tatchilla snapped. "Don't be a skimmer. You weren't flogging the wind for that cloud bank because you thought the aliens had come to trade metals."

Farsight said, "We have so far counted twelve home crystals known to be destroyed or at least missing, far from their presumed stations."

That made Jardbrass gulp. But he was not prepared to go beyond his particular concern. "Just the same, this ship and the attached alien box are within our jurisdiction. You will submit to our elected council, or you may move off."

It was unbelievable. Tatchilla came back with some obscure legal point. One of the Polars cited a long-ago precedent. And in a flash the entire perch echoed with the sound of wrangling.

People are what they are. They have their limits, I guess. I was trying to be philosophical, but it was getting hard. I was acutely aware of the fact that Lackofa was boxed up in the Crate, sweating and deep-breathing. And that Aguella was docked, wounded, no doubt feeling abandoned.

Deep worms, shut up, I said silently. Only when I saw the shocked stares and heard the sudden silence did I realize I'd said it out loud.

chapter 12

Too late to take it back. And anyway, I didn't want to take it back. Squabbling wasn't going to win the game.

"There are more Capasin ships," I said. "They're here to exterminate us. They'll be back. You need to conceal your home crystal in the clouds for as long as you can. And start building weapons."

"Who . . . what are you?" Jardbrass demanded.

I started to answer, but a new voice interrupted. "He's the only one who is playing the game." It was Menno. How had I missed those oversized wings?

"This is not a game," Jardbrass said in a freezing voice intended to silence the uppity youngsters.

"Yes, it is," Menno insisted, completely unintimidated. "It is a game, and the Capasins think it's a game, and if we don't play — we lose. It's why they've come. They've come to play. They've come at our invitation."

Jardbrass started to speak. But no words came. He collapsed all at once. The hard set of his face, his determined expression, all dissolved. "Twelve crystals?" he whispered pitifully. "It cannot be."

"What does he mean 'at our invitation'?" Farsight asked Menno directly.

Menno didn't answer. He smiled at me, a haunted shadow of the cocky gamer I'd met at the Dance By.

I knew what he meant. I knew what they had done. "They've found a way to wave broadcast," I said. "But it must have been fairly recently. How could wave broadcasts have traveled so far off-world and reached the Capasins?"

"We linked to a Zero-space transponder," Menno said proudly. "We're a century ahead of you Equatorials, you know. We can punch a signal through the background radiation. And we can bounce it through Z-space. In ten years we'd have had a full airfoil crystal and been the hub of a global uninet. And soon thereafter we could have linked directly to the Generationals and the Illamans on their home worlds. It would have been a revolution!"

"What signals did you bounce through Z-space, Polar?" I asked.

"Can't you guess, my Equatorial friend? Simple mathematical formulas at first, for the earliest tests. But we had to see whether the system could handle heavy data traffic."

"Mother Sky, you broadcast games! You bounced games through Z-space."

"Yes. Brilliant, wasn't it?" Menno sneered. "Except for the slight, small fact, that some species don't know the difference between games and reality. These aliens are here to exterminate us because they've seen our games and believe them to be real. They think we make toys of other species. That we interfere with their development with utter indifference to the results. They aren't here to do evil. They're here to annihilate what they believe to be a race of murderers."

This horrifying news was still ringing in the stunned silence when someone cried, "Look!"

Every head turned.

Two Capasin ships emerged from the clouds. I didn't wait for orders; I beat wing to the Crate.

I slid down through the hatch and barreled into Lackofa. "They're —" I panted.

"I saw them!"

"Fifty percent thrust!"

I grabbed the controls as we shot away from the EmCee. Which target? Left or right? Left was closest to the Polar Orbit High. Stop them first, then —

A beam of light sliced the nub of a wing from the Polar. A chunk of new crystal fell, dragging thirty or more Ketrans down with it. Who had fired? Behind us! On top of us!

I spun the Crate, let momentum carry us skimming beneath the belly of the ship, and fired right up into it.

At the same moment the other two Capasin ships blazed with flechettes. The tiny shrapnel caught the Polars from two sides. Maybe someone lived through that. But not enough to provide even a semblance of lift.

It was my home all over again. Only this time no desperate wings fought gravity. This time the docked males and females, juvies and oldsters, were all nothing more than ballast. Dead weight.

Polar Orbit High Crystal fell like an unstrung corpse. Simply fell from the sky.

The Capasin ship above us veered off, having now seen the peril that we represented. Too late to matter. Polar Orbit High was gone. And it was three Capasin ships against the EmCee's force field and the Crate's pitiful weapons.

No winning move. Nothing left but to fly away. Retreat. A valid strategy; I had seen many a species retreat from an attack, regroup, renumber, resurge.

Fly away.

"Reverse thrust," I said.

Lackofa didn't respond.

"It's the only move, Lackofa. The Crate. We have to save it. It's the only weapon we have. Our only chance."

"They'll kill everyone. Everyone, won't they? Every crystal, one by one."

"Not us," I said harshly. "Not if we run. Lackofa, we're it. We're all we have now. All of the Ketran race. Now reverse thrust. Do it."

The Capasin ships didn't bother to pursue us as the EmCee and we two in the Crate blew toward space. High above our lost, doomed planet we rendezvoused with the EmCee and were accepted back inside the force field.

It was the end of Ket. And, although there were still seventy-two Ketrans alive at that moment, it was also the end of my race.

SECOND LIFE

chapter 13

"Commander, the system appears to have six true planets and nine moons. Two of the moons — both orbiting the second planet — may be habitable. None of the planets."

I nodded. "We'll go take a look. Fields at full power, passive sensors to maximum range, active sensors off, fighters to alert status two."

My words became actions. The ship's defensive force field shimmered, distorting my view of the system's sun and the stars beyond. A probe extruded through the field to gather every bit of electronic data available. Our active sensors, what we called the "pingers," were shut down: They could alert possible enemies to our presence. And far down in the waist of the ship three wing-tied pilots slid into the snug cockpits of heavily armed fighters, and keyed up engine and weapons power. Nine more pilots remained at ready station, prepared to go hostile in less than three minutes.

It was the seventy-ninth time we had entered a system and carried out our search for a home. The days and years of excitement were long since past.

It was a routine now. It was what we did. Hope and disappointment and all the rest of the emotional baggage had slowly drained away, failure after bitter failure.

We had learned to expect nothing. We'd learned to discount every encouraging datum and to believe every ill omen. Seventy-nine systems in sixty-three years. And that was only the systems worth investigation. How many other systems had we visited solely for the purpose of mining mineral-rich asteroids, or to accumulate hydrogen?

It was what we did. It was who we were now. The Ket: less than a hundred wanderers in search of a new home.

We had encountered several sentient species. Some space-faring, most not. Some pitied us. Some attacked us. But we'd learned to defend ourselves in these last sixty-three years. We began with the Capasin Crate, copying its weapons. Then came improvements, innovations.

The MCQ3 had mutated over the years to become the Searcher, and the Searcher was a very different ship. A close examination would still reveal the original crystal formation at the heart of her, but most of what had been added was dull titanium and mineral-polymer composites. The original Z-space engines had long since been replaced, and new, fast sub-Z engines had been added as well.

Two stubby wings gave us an airfoil for penetrating atmosphere. And the weapons arrays beneath each wing, and the even dozen stubby black fighters, earned us the respect of potential foes.

"Fields up, Commander," Menno reported.

"We'll try the blue one first," I said. I saw Aguella smile. I had been the commander since Farsight died, some fifty years ago. But I still resisted referring to every planet or moon by its proper sequential designation.

Aguella was docked, eyes closed to focus on the sensor readout. Her wings beat slowly, regularly. Pointlessly, too, since no one in more than six decades had beat wing for lift.

And yet, we were still Ketran. We still wanted to fly.

"The blue one it is, Commander," Menno confirmed.

Menno was my second-in-command, the subcommander. It was a compromise. We had come very close to civil war at one point. Menno and the fugitive Polars and some of the dazed, confused refugees we'd saved from a shattered Tropical Midrange Low had banded together to demand a democratic form of government aboard the Searcher. Of course it was more about resisting Equatorial dominance than anything else.

Democracy was not possible on a ship in hostile space. But compromise was. The compromise was Menno. He held second dock. And he did his job very well, though he and I would never be friends.

It had become very personal. For Menno it was just another game he had to win at all costs. I didn't deceive myself: He was playing that game still. And if he ever took my place he would have no votes: He would command.

We slipped into high orbit above the blue moon.

"It's water," Aguella said. Her tone showed only the slightest trace of disappointment. We had learned that planets with a large amount of water never provided the updrafts, or the atmospheric pressures we needed to sustain our crystal-based civilization.

Just that quickly the blue moon became useless to us. It was not a great surprise. I suppressed a disappointed sigh. The people looked to me. I had to set an example. My youth was long since gone and I carried too many responsibilities to be self-indulgent.

"Navigator, lay an intercept course for the white one," I ordered.

"Wait!"

It was Aguella. I glanced at her and saw intense

focus on her face. I keyed up the sensor displays; Menno did the same. But whatever she had seen, neither of us spotted it.

I *memmed* her. "What is it?"

She broke out two displays and highlighted them for the benefit of Menno and me. When this still failed to move me, she said impatiently, "There's something moving . . . floating. In the water, through the water. Beneath the surface. See the light? There, on the dark side. A light pattern, highly refracted, of course."

"What's the other display?" Menno asked.

"Water current. See? The . . . the thing, whatever it is, is moving against the current. And it's putting off light."

"A large fish with chemically produced light?" I suggested. "We've seen that before."

"Probably," Aguella agreed. "But maybe not. I can't say anything for sure but I had the impression, nothing more than an impression, that I was seeing a complex structure."

"Crystalline?" Menno asked, disapproving.

"I don't know," Aguella snapped. "Not without using active sensors."

"Too dangerous. Too much risk for what possible reward?" Menno argued. "Are you suggesting we should light up this ship on the off chance that someone, somewhere down there is living some watery mockery of our own long-dead lives? We don't breathe water, Aguella. We don't fly in water. This is all just pointless obsession with the past."

The last remark was guaranteed to outrage Aguella. And it was intended to provoke me. I quickly *memmed* Aguella to stay silent.

In my mildest voice I said, "This ship's mission remains clearly defined, Menno."

"Yes, to wander the galaxy in search of what we now know to be the rarest of all environments," he shot back. "We've adapted in a dozen ways, but never in this. We have enclosed fighters, and we've learned to live with that. We've long since dropped even the pretence of flying for lift. But we refuse to accept the obvious: There will never be another Ket. No more home crystals. Dozens of planets and what do we find, again and again? Surface dwellers. Surface dwellers. Nothing but surface dwellers."

"We are of the skies!" Aguella erupted. "We do not crawl. We do not walk. We are born to a life in the skies!"

"We're dying for that myth. No one has juvies anymore. We're dying out as a race, all for some vision of a world that no longer exists."

That last was a shard meant for Aguella and me. We were a declared couple, but we'd never sired. It had become an unwritten rule of our strange, cut-off, castaway civilization that we would bring no new lives into being till we had a home.

"That's enough," I said, calling a halt to the dissension before it spread to the other crew. "This ship has a mission. Menno, we'll take a look at this subaqueous phenomenon of Aguella's. No, not with active sensors. We'll take Jicklet's new Explorer. It's time we tested her."

"I'll take the search team of course," Menno said with just the faint hint of a smirk. He knew I didn't trust him in command of the Searcher. He was letting me know that he knew how I felt.

"Actually, I'll command the search team. It's been some time since I made planetfall. Menno, you'll assume temporary command here. Aguella, you're with me. *Memm* to Lackofa and Jicklet to join us. And *memm* Third Officer Deeved to take sensor station here."

Menno nodded. I had called his bluff. I'd demonstrated that I was sufficiently confident to leave him in charge. At least as long as I brought Deeved to the perch as well. Deeved was third officer, a Tropical. He was no ally of mine, but he despised Menno. Menno wouldn't get away with anything while Deeved was around.

I hated the atmosphere of suspicion and mistrust, but I'd adapted. It was why command was now centered in this perch where we could all see each other in real space: Any of our functions could have been carried out from dock, through the ship's uninet. But in a world where betrayal was a real possibility it was reassuring to be able to stay globes to globes. I needed to see Menno. And I enjoyed seeing Aguella.

I flew down-ship with Aguella close beside me. Lackofa met us halfway to the Explorer.

"You're leaving Menno in charge, Ellimist? Are you crazy? He'll turn this ship around and head back to his little Utopia."

Lackofa steadfastly refused to either treat me with the deference due to an official Wise One, or the obedience due a commander, or for that matter the basic respect due to any fellow Ketran. I valued him all the more.

He had grown cranky over the years. Crankier even than when he'd been a lowly third biologist. He was the ship's chief scientist.

"I have Deeved watching him. And anyway, the crew is loyal."

Lackofa said, "Don't count too much on loyalty, Ellimist. It's a weak force."

He was not being merely facetious. He was serious. Did he know something?

I wanted to press him for information, but Lack-ofa was trusted by every faction. He was trusted precisely because it was known that he would never violate a confidence or become an informer.

And yet he was sending me a clear signal. Most likely he was exaggerating. Most likely.

chapter 14

Too late to turn back now without showing unacceptable weakness. No choice but to go forward
and count on a divided, faction-riven crew and
what Lackofa called the weak force of loyalty.

The Explorer was a new ship whose design
reflected lessons learned in previous encounters
with alien craft. Jicklet and her people had been at
work on her for five years. The basic materials had
been drawn from asteroids and from occasional
planetfalls. Jicklet had something of an empire now:
a large yet cramped complex of shops, foundries,
fuelers, hangers, and repair cradles. Ugly crystal and
metal structures formed a clunky, asymmetrical ring
around the ship, below the fighter stations and
above the engines.

Jicklet handled the engines, the weapons and
the small craft. If there was anyone with more
power than the commander, it was Head Tech Jicklet. But in her at least, loyalty was not a weak force.

I had toured the Explorer in its various stages of
construction and presided at a ceremony of launch-

ing. I was familiar with the ship, but it had rested, unused, in its cradle for the last year.

Jicklet was practically vibrating with anticipation.

"Head Tech, I hate to call on you at such short notice. You know, you're welcome to send one of your subs along if you're otherwise occupied."

A joke, of course. No power in the galaxy could have kept her from flying the Explorer's first mission.

"I think I can make the time," Jicklet said dryly. "May I ask the mission?"

"That watery moon down there. We want to take a look below the surface without using active sensors."

"The Explorer will handle it," she said confidently.

It was a pretty craft, a nice melding of Ketran sensibilities and alien pragmatism. A crate, but largely transparent, with flat-crys panels buttressed by force fields. She was not Z-space capable, designed for O and A: Orbit and Atmosphere. There were swooped wings and massive ion propulsion engines at the back. She was fast, versatile, and heavily armed with our own improved version of the Capasin beam weapon, as well as a number of fire-and-forget explosive homers.

So many weapons. So much killing power.

I put on an approving smile for Jicklet's benefit, but she'd seen my doubts.

"We've come a long way through a dangerous galaxy," she said.

"A long way," I agreed. We had lost our world because the Capasins thought we were aggressors when we were not. What was the moral of that story? That we should be prepared for violence at every turn? Right or wrong, that was the lesson we had learned. We would never be unprepared again.

And yet, here we were displaying our readiness for mayhem in every curve of our ship. Were we setting ourselves up for another, even more complete annihilation?

No time for all that. I needed to clear my mind of possible betrayal and possible wrong impressions. Focus on the mission at hand.

"Let's see what your toy can do, Jicklet."

We went aboard and docked. We were enclosed but able to see stars in every direction but down. A compromise. Just what Menno had in mind for our race: adaptation. If no planet matched our needs, maybe we should match ourselves to the planet. We had the genetic manipulation techniques to do it in a few generations. We oldsters would live out our lives as pitiful, flightless Ketrans. But our juvies would be born without wings, with sturdier builds, stronger bones, true feet instead of pods, and no docking talons at all.

Was Menno right?

No. Not while I was commander.

The Explorer released its hold on the Searcher and Jicklet lit the engines. The g forces accumulated but the internal force fields supported our weight, even kept the blood from pooling in our extremities.

We raced for the blue moon and used the thin atmosphere for braking. We had to shed nearly all of our speed before we could safely enter the water. The Explorer skimmed at subsonic speeds, just ten feet above the glass-smooth sea.

"Any particular target?" Jicklet asked Aguella.

"Ahead nine miles. That should bring us to an intercept with the phenomenon I observed."

We crossed the day-night line and Jicklet killed the last of our speed. The ship sliced the water in a shallow angle.

There was an immediate sensation of claustrophobia. One cannot be raised on a floating airborne crystal, spend decades in a ship surrounded by a billion miles of open space, and then feel entirely calm about being plunged into the enveloping sea.

The water closed in all around us, dark, soon nearly opaque. Then, Jicklet keyed the lights and I gasped. A school of thousands of brilliant yellow eels, myriad bars of shimmering light, flew past us, around us.

"Phosphorescence," Lackofa commented. "That may be all you saw, Aguella: a school of eels."

"But beautiful eels," I remarked.

The yellow swarm passed us by and now, no longer blinded by them, I saw wonders of light and motion everywhere. A fish nearly the size of the Explorer with gaping mouth and feathery fins, all bright with neon reds and blues; a creature that looked like an airfoil trailing a tangle of purple tentacles; a flight of seven or eight fish, long, dangerous-looking, brightest pink; and below us a forest of very long tentacles, so long they disappeared down out of sight.

A blur of movement!

The Explorer rocked, tilted sharply, and with a deep, groaning sound, stopped.

"Something has us, Commander!" Jicklet yelled.

She was more concerned than I. It was "her" ship, after all, and she treasured every square inch of it.

"All external lights up. Active sensors on. Weapons to full ready. Jicklet: We'll give it a jolt of current through the hull if need be."

"Ready, Commander," Jicklet replied.

The external lights doubled in brilliance. The water was wonderfully clear but we were still in planetary night and the lights failed to show the full extent of the tendrils or whatever it was that had us wrapped securely. The eels and fish still swam serenely by.

"Sensor readouts coming in," Aguella said. "Lifeform. Carbon-based." She frowned.

"What?" I asked.

"The creature that has us appears to be quite large. Unless I'm getting false readings I show a continuous nervous-electrical system extending out to the limits of the sensors. This thing extends beyond the horizon. In every direction!"

I did a quick mental calculation, the circumference of the moon, distance to horizon . . .

"It has to be a sensor glitch," I said. "Nothing is that big."

"We're moving," Lackofa pointed out quite dispassionately.

I had already felt the motion. We were being drawn lower.

"Okay. Shock the hull," I ordered.

The lights dimmed as power was diverted into the hull's metallic components. Anything in contact with us would receive a severe jolt.

"It still has us," Lackofa pointed out unnecessarily.

"Understood," I said. "Beam to minimum power.

Wide pattern." I was still calm. I regretted having to take harsher measures. Most likely this life-form was sub-sentient, simply a creature following its instincts. But the ship came first.

"Fire."

The beam fired. The water absorbed most of the energy, particularly at this setting, but the creature would still feel searing, intense heat.

The water steamed and boiled around us.

"Cease fire. Report."

"It still has us," Lackofa said. "A creature this large may not even have pain receptors in an area this small. It may not feel us."

I nodded. "We'll have to cut our way out. Beam to tight focus. Mid-power. Jicklet, give us a sweep below the hull. We'll slice the tentacles off. As soon as we're free you'd better take us back to atmosphere."

"Understood."

The beam fired, a lance of light inscribing a brilliant circle beneath us.

The Explorer shuddered as the tentacles fell away. The ship began to rise.

"Something close!" Aguella yelled.

"Commander!" Jicklet cried.

The monster slammed us head on. I was knocked off my dock. My talons were wrenched and bleed-

110

ing. Aguella and Jicklet were still docked but Lack-ofa was down, out cold. Huge! A flash of monstrous mouth, wide enough to swallow the ship in a single bite.

"Beam to maximum. Fire!"

The vast mouth was lit red. An explosion rocked the fish, its insides, superheated, had blown apart, ripping it open.

Wham!

Wham!

I staggered up. My face was wet with my own blood now.

Wham!

Lights. Blinded. Trying to think, trying to form the order.

"Missiles! Fire!"

No answer.

Wham!

Hammer blows, one after another. The force field maintained hull integrity, but we were bugs inside a bean pod being slammed again and again.

Lights gone. No sound. Silence. I lay broken and battered. Head swirling.

Water rushing in. How? The fields should have . . .

Something touching me. My face. Touching me, wrapping itself around me and . . .

chapter 15

I was docked.

Sky. All around me.

The crystal!

I was docked to a crystal. Azure Level. Docked, eyes open, yet in the game. I was playing Inidar. The game scenario involved two alien species, one a wandering nomad race in search of a new home. The other species was a world-sized behemoth. So vast, so all-consuming that it very nearly was the planet.

"I'll take the Ketrans, if you choose to accept."

"Gladly," Inidar *memmed* back. "You underestimate the value of size and power. You're an idealist, Ellimist."

"Oh? Well, step into my lair, said the *dreth* to the *chorkant.*"

Inidar laughed.

"Shall we immerse?"

"On the other side," he answered.

"This isn't real," I *memmed.* "You're dead, Inidar. You died a long time ago."

"True enough, Ellimist," he agreed. "The Capasin killed me. Killed us all. They're here, too, you know. Would you like to see them?"

"The Capasin? Where? Where is 'here'?"

"Open your eyes, Ellimist, what do you see?"

"Equatorial High Crystal. But she's dead, too. And Lackofa in the next dock. Is he dead? Am I dead? Or is this some kind of dream? Hallucination?"

"Are those the only choices?" Inidar asked, mocking. "Might it not be a game?"

"It might," I said. "But whose?"

Inidar laughed delightedly in my head. Then he was gone, and before me, before my eyes, not a uninet *memm,* but right in front of me appeared the Capasin. The one I had killed.

"Hello again, Ellimist," he said. There was a gaping, bloody wound in the top of his head and down where the point of the crystal shard had extruded from his throat.

"This is all a trick," I said.

"Yes. Almost as neat a trick as the way you skewered me. A primitive spear to stop a modern spacecraft. Ouch!"

"What is this game?" I demanded. I was not the juvie I appeared to be, I was commander of the Searcher. I was commander of all that remained of the Ketran people. All that remained.

"Well, whose fault is that?" the Capasin asked as if he'd read my thoughts. "You invent games where you play with the lives of entire species, you cleverly broadcast these games through Z-space without bothering to include the explanation that they are games, just games. And then you're surprised when someone comes along to squash you like so many parasites."

"You didn't exactly wait for explanations," I snapped. "You slaughtered us."

The Capasin spread his limp arms in a very Ketran gesture. "It's what we do. And if you'd had any fortitude you'd have returned and taken your planet back. Instead you wander around lost, looking for a place that doesn't exist. You're a cowardly species."

"Less than a hundred of us in one ship to retake Ket?" I sneered. "You sound like Menno. It was always the radical move with him: Return and fight it out to the death, or adapt and become something entirely new."

"Yes, and now we see how right I was," Menno said. He was crowding in beside the dead Capasin, elbowing him aside. "Look where you've got us. Do you even know? We're the game pieces now. Father has us. Father has gathered us here, made us into his toys."

"What are you talking about?"

"You think it's all a dream, don't you, Ellimist? It's real. Or mostly real. Inidar is a construct, a fake built out of your own memories. So is this one particular Capasin, though there are real Capasins here. And anyway, I'm real enough. In my own way."

"Why are you here? You should be aboard the Searcher."

"I was in command, remember? Not you. We saw when you went to active sensors. At that point I ordered the same, no reason not to. So we saw you firing weapons down there. I took the Searcher down to rescue you. Surprised, eh? Surprised that I would try and save your life? Don't be. How could I abandon you and hope to maintain control of the crew? No one wins the game of assassination. I had to at least try and rescue you."

"The Searcher can't penetrate a water environment," I said suspiciously.

"Father's reach goes beyond the water," Menno said. "He controls everything on this moon. We were skimming the surface, trying frantically to fit out one of the fighters to go in after you. And all at once a wall of water — impossible, of course — it rose up from nowhere, a wave a half mile high. And you're right: The Searcher doesn't do well in water."

"Aguella?" I asked.

"Right here," she said.

"How did you . . . Are you all right?"

"I was killed, Toomin. We all were. All but you."

I wanted to laugh. It was ludicrous. She was talking, she was right there now, in front of my face. Hovering in the pure clean air of home.

"Would you like to see the truth, Ellimist?" Menno asked.

"Yes, of course."

"Don't be so quick to decide. You won't like the truth."

"You're all dead. What can be worse?"

Menno's smile spread wide.

And all at once the crystal was gone, the sky gone. I was underwater. Underwater but breathing. Something held me. Tentacles. Deep worms, they were inside me! The tendrils grew into me, penetrated me, made me a part of them.

I floated, tethered, in a field of tentacles that spread as far as the eye could see. Menno floated nearby, tethered, penetrated, incorporated. His eyes were closed. His chest had burst open. I could see his insides.

A few feet away — Aguella. My lovely Aguella. Tied. Attached. A dead thing grafted onto the creature called Father.

Lackofa. Jicklet. Bodies, more and more, I twisted to see more and more. They were all around me, some seemingly uninjured, others torn apart by impact wounds or by sudden depressurization.

Everywhere the dead. The last of the Ketran people.

"No, you are the last of the Ketran people, Toomin the Ellimist," Aguella said.

She was before me once more, hovering, her beautiful face, her . . . all an illusion. The crystal floated. The people lifted. Far below, the lava rivers ran.

"What do you want with us?" I cried.

"I am Father," Lackofa said. He was gazing down at me from his dock above. Old Forty-two. "I am the life of this planet. All that is here comes from me, belongs to me, is a part of me. All power is mine."

I had a sudden, searing glimpse, a compressed data file downloaded at ten times normal speed, like a hundred *memms* exploding in my head at once. I saw Father. He covered every square inch of the moon, every mile of ocean floor, every tiny island, everything from pole to pole. A billion tentacles all waving and waiting.

We were not Father's only victims. I saw Generationals and Illamans. I saw Capasins. I saw members of races we had encountered on our long, long search. I saw races no Ketran had ever met. All of them dead. None alive but me, if this was truly life.

But it mattered little to Father. Even the dead could be used, kept whole, their soulless brains made to function.

How many spacecraft had been drawn to this blue moon? Father was old. He had been old before the first sentient lit his first rocket.

"What do you want with me?" I cried.

Menno said, "It is lonely with only the dead for company. I want to play a game, Ellimist."

chapter 16

The game was all.

Aguella was gone. Dead. For the first few years — decades? centuries? — Father had brought her to me. She had come and Lackofa had come and Menno had come. All my dead brothers and sisters, my friends, my enemies, my love. All dead. But still Father had given me my home in Azure Level, my old home, with my fellows around me. Inidar was there, and Wormer, built of my own memory.

The pure memories, those that Father created out of my mind, were thin, paltry creatures. They did only what they had always done. It was a shame I had never known them better. If my memories had gone deeper Father could have made them more amusing.

Where Father had the body and brain he could be far more creative. Aguella and I propagated. We had three juvies. But they were sad illusions, partial, incomplete: I had never paid any attention to young juvies. My mind could not create them, write them fully. They seemed to come and go at random. I would remember them and they would appear; I would forget them and they would disappear for hours or days.

Lackofa and I grew old together, old friends. We spent our free time together. Recited the old poems together, talked about the good old days. He grew old. So did I.

Jicklet would come by sometimes. We would run into her at the perches. She was quite the respected person now, under consideration for appointment to the Council.

And Menno? For a while it was Menno I played against in every game. Father would match us together. Father enjoyed watching the interaction of hostilities. Menno and I were so different. But over time our hostility paled, faded. It's hard to hate a dead person. Even one who seems so vital and alive.

How many games had I played with Father? A thousand? Ten thousand? I tried to refuse, but when I did he simply turned off the illusion of home and I saw who and what and where I was. I was back under the sea, tethered for eternity to the tendril that grew inside me, that reached itself into my brain. I was back amidst the endless forest of tentacles with Lackofa and Menno and poor Aguella still floating, dead but never decaying, never disintegrating, never, never at peace.

But it was more than the loss of illusions that motivated me to play. It was that I had nothing else. Nothing but the game.

The game and the tiny flicker of undying hope.

What a sad, desperate illusion. How ludicrous to cling to the hope of escape. And escape to what? Where would I go? What would I be? I was part of Father. There was no Toomin, no Ellimist. There was only Father.

And yet . . . I still lived. I still played the game and made my own gaming decisions.

Father needed me, I had long since recognized that fact. He kept me alive to play. Because though I lost each game, I was his best opponent.

"I want to play a game," Father said. He had acquired a new face, his own face, or a facsimile, a sort of "game name." He took Ketran form, an oldster, a Wise One. He flew to my dock, hovered, and repeated, "Shall we immerse?"

"On the other side," I said.

Father played many games. Many games. I believe he had culled them from a thousand races, all over the galaxy. We had played games not much different than our own old Alien Civilizations. We had simple games of reflex. Killing games. Games of forethought involving the complex movement of

121

pieces on a flat plane or within a cube or within n-dimensional space. Games that were games of games.

It was all I had. I had begged Father to kill me, to end it. But of course he refused. I had tried deliberately losing, hoping to make the games boring to Father. But Father was patient: He could outwait me. For years, decades, it didn't matter to him. And in the end I always came back to the game.

You make what you can of the life you have, I suppose.

The new game began.

It was different. Father had acquired some new species.

I was all at once in a close, dank, almost airless room. At least it seemed airless to me, a Ketran. Though in all fairness I now lived out my life smothered beneath miles of ocean and tethered to a tendril so I was hardly one to complain.

Nevertheless, it seemed airless. Not a large room, perhaps a hundred feet square. There were creatures, odd, misshapen things that seemed to be an amalgamation of a dozen different races. Faces with two eyes front and a third eye facing back. Their hair was long, running all the way down their spiked backs to the floor. All different colors: green hair and red hair and yellow. Black faces and white and purple. Arms seemed to be almost optional; some had three, others as many as nine.

They were definitely new. Like no race I'd ever seen before. Father had made a new acquisition.

I knew instinctively that we were aboard a ship. But it moved. Not the smooth acceleration of a spacecraft. This ship moved up and down and sideways as if it were being buffeted by a storm, or even floating on a watery sea.

The creatures sat at tables with their individualistic bodies splayed out comfortably. They were enjoying drinks. Perhaps mild intoxicants. And they were watching us.

We, me and Father in the person of Menno, were performers at one end of the room on a raised platform. We each held a tool of some sort. A long thing, nearly my own body length, a sort of flattened, whimsically shaped board. And stretched along the board were seven taut strings. There was a mouthpiece as well that reached up to where I could, by bending my neck just a little, place it in my mouth.

Menno grinned at me, a cocky challenge. He placed his mouth around the mouthpiece and blew while strumming his fingers across the strings.

The result . . . it was . . . it was like nothing I'd heard in life or a dream.

The sounds were not mere sounds. I don't have words to explain. Maybe no one does. The sounds touched a part of me I'd long forgotten. The sounds made me think of Aguella. Of home. Of the stars and the sun and the clouds and of all the beauty, sadness, joy, and laughter I'd ever known.

Menno/Father finished playing and the creatures in the audience emitted honking vocalizations that seemed especially harsh in contrast with the sounds of Menno's instrument.

"Your turn," Menno said.

I placed my lips as I'd seen him do, and my hands as he had done. And I made sounds. But not the sounds he had made. Mine were harsh and grating and contemptible in my own ears.

And yet, I could hear, even there, even in my own incoherence, the seed of something. Something.

The audience favored me with stony silence.

"That's game." Menno laughed.

"What is this game, Father?"

"These creatures are called the Unemites. They are not space-faring. I happened to draw a Skrit Na freighter into my web — useless species, the Skrit Na — and aboard their ship they had a Unemite captive."

"The game, Father. What is it called?"

"They call it music."

"I can never hope to win," I said. "I beg you, Father: Release me. I don't want to play it again."

He refused. Of course I knew he would. And I knew this about Father: His one weakness was his cruelty. I could use that. He would force me to play this game a thousand times.

Step into my lair, said the *dreth* to the *chorkant*.

chapter 17

"Shall we immerse?"

"On the other side," I answered.

The Unemites. The instruments. The hundredth game.

I had waited. So hard to show just enough improvement to entice Father, to challenge him, without revealing all that I was learning. So hard to lay the foundation of this moment.

The hundredth game. But the ten thousandth time I had played it in my mind, all alone. The instrument, the *adge*, as the Unemites called it, had scarcely been out of my thoughts.

The *adge* had become a part of me. It was inside me, in my brain, and even if Father ended the game, he could never take the adge from me, never take music from me, never. I owned it. I had become it. And now, this game, the hundredth, I would show him.

He was Menno, cocky, sure of victory, but wary enough that he had to try harder than he'd have liked to gain the approval of the audience.

And yet, in a hundred games Father had not advanced. Not an original idea, not a new expression. Ironic at some level: Menno, the real Ketran Menno, had always been an advocate of taking the game to a new level, injecting a wild disregard for convention.

I smiled to myself. *Ah, Menno, you'd be proud of me.*

But it was Aguella who was in my thoughts as I raised the adge's mouthpiece to my lips. It was Aguella who made the music possible for me, and the lack of an Aguella, or anything like her, that would doom poor Father. You needed love to win at the game of music.

I played a riff. Menno gaped. The audience sat forward.

That's right, Father, I've rewritten the rules.

I played of sadness. I played of loneliness. Despair. Love found and lost. I played of tragic misunderstanding and weary cynicism and defeat. I played of perseverance, endurance beyond all suffering. Endurance in the face of hopelessness, hope when even hope was a betrayal.

My *adge* spoke of every terrible moment of my life. It spoke of the loss of my people. The loss of friends. Losses and losses.

And yet, though I played so much sadness, the music at the same time denied despair. How could anyone despair while music was being played?

I could see it in the Unemite faces: They heard the loneliness and in that expression of loneliness found comfort for their own.

Oh, yes, I had them. I owned them, the audience. I had them through and through and they would go with me wherever my adge led.

And Father? Oh, it was sweet to see him. Sweet to watch his uneasiness turn to amazement turn to sullen anger.

The music didn't touch him. But he could see that I had won. I had won the game so resoundingly, so finally that he could never hope to compete with me again. Not at the game of music.

"How?" he asked me finally.

I played a phrase on my *adge,* and then I did what no Unemite had conceived of doing. I sang. I used my voice, my Ketran voice, to make the sounds that the adge could not.

The Unemites went mad. The hooting was frantic, manic, insane. Lovely.

"How?!" Menno/Father demanded, barely concealing the rage.

"I'm a loser," I sang in answer. "They called me a brilliant loser, all winners, all winners but me: loser. But only a loser can sing the azures. Only a loser truly sees."

chapter 18

I thought that Father would kill me straightaway. But he didn't.

I thought he would never play the game of music again, but he tried. And this time he copied much of what I'd done. It didn't matter. I had a new trick up my sleeve: improvisation.

I had devised a tactic of improvising in duet. I would offer a musical phrase, play for a few moments, then invite him to pick up the thread and extrapolate.

Father could not. And his efforts were pitiful.

For a long time afterward, Father did not approach me. No games of any kind. Nothing but silence. I was left to float, left to gaze out across the grim sea of tethered, invaded bodies. Long-dead Aguella. My muse.

But everything was changed now. I had music. And even without an *adge* I was so long-used to living inside my own mind that I could play and compose all the endless days and nights.

At long last, after years perhaps, Father came to me. He had a new game, a new species. Not music, not anything like it. A simple game of placement and pieces.

I lost the first four games. I won the fifth. The sixth. The next five games after that. Every game.

Father raged and twisted the scenario into a nightmare vision. He stormed away and left me to float.

And surely now he would kill me. He understood what had happened. I had won at music and that free-form, improvisational game had done things to my mind, changed me in ways even I could not understand. I saw in more dimensions. Intuition was close to me now, intimate to me. I trusted my own moves. And conversely, Father had been shaken.

A year. A new game. A killing game this time. Weapons in a maze.

I won the first game.

I won every game.

Silence from Father. Why did he not kill me?

I reached out to him, wanted to know his mind. But he made no answer. He had gone far away, he had withdrawn. And yet, I lived.

And then dreadful hope, that awful emotion that draws us to our doom, began to rise in me. I reached out, reached down my tether, through Father's own neural net as if it was a biological uninet. I reached for Aguella.

"Aguella. My love."

"Toomin?"

"Yes."

"Am I alive?"

"Do you think? Do you see? Do you sense?"

"I . . ."

I could see her dead body, see her through the sun-dappled water. See her through a passing cloud of neon-green fish.

"My memories, all . . ." she said. "I feel you, Toomin. Only you. Alive, but . . . what is happening?"

So many years, how could my heart still tear apart? How could the pain still be so fresh?

"You live in my memory, Aguella. But now, here, in this place, you live only when Father touches your neurons, when he raises your memories."

"There is no Father, here," she said.

"I have made you live again, for this moment. The parts of you that I touch come alive again, Aguella. The memories, the notions, the ideas. But only for the moment."

"Then I am dead."

"Yes. You are gone, Aguella. This is only the shadow of you, the biological brain, neurons switched on, a biological computer, nothing more."

"Let me see. Once more, let me see what I am."

"No. No."

"Ah."

"Aguella. I . . ."

Could I ask permission? Of a person dead for decades? It was a mockery. She would give the answer I sought. Her will was long gone, long since flown away.

"I am making you a part of me, Aguella. Do you understand? I am downloading you, your thoughts, your knowledge. All that you were. Are."

"I was always a part of you, and you a part of me."

I lowered the barriers between us. Felt the flood of information come into me. Data, that's all it was, the encoded data that, deciphered, was all that made her Ketran. Her fear, her desire, her love.

It all became a part of me and even in that terrible moment, that hideous moment when I treated my one love like nothing more than a uninet file, I gloated and thought, *Ah, Father, you were a fool to withdraw. Now I'll come for you.*

I downloaded Jicklet. Lackofa. Menno. One by one I absorbed their minds.

The other Ketrans, till all the last of the Ketrans were inside me.

And then others. Alien minds. Alien thoughts.

Alien sights. Faster! Generationals. Illamans. Capasins. Skrit Na. More! Faster!

I was a uninet bug, eating data, spreading, consuming, absorbing. Still I was no more than one percent of Father, but already I was a hundred times myself.

Daankins, 333's, the Wurb, the Breets, the Multitude, the Chan Wath. Race after race. I emptied each dead mind into mine, each set of data, no time to look, to see, to open and enjoy, oh no, no time, the race was on, a race to consume, to download and absorb.

How long till you see it, Father? How long till you spot this new game?

On and on I roared. And still Father did not feel me, did not sense his growing peril. Why should he? Father had never known a true enemy. He had owned his entire world for his entire evolution. A single life-form that had invented every other that swam in his sea, simply to amuse himself.

Then, at long last, I felt his unease. Felt his attention. He sent out impulses, racing through his vast network, felt here and there for the cause of the odd, disturbing sensation.

I showed him nothing. I hid myself. He searched and found only emptiness. Emptiness where there had been captive minds. Where were the Capasins? Where were the Generationals? Where were the Graspers?

Where were those Ketrans?

And at long last, as his slow-growing dread emerged, as he began to feel a new emotion, he asked: Where is Ellimist?

I was half of Father now. We were equal. I stopped my advance.

"Shall we immerse, Father?" I said.

"What game?" he demanded.

"The game, Father. The last game."

THIRD LIFE

chapter 19

The last mind I absorbed was Father himself. And when I took him, I took nothing.

There was no Father. No mind at all. He was nothing but a sponge, in the end. A creature of the simplest biology, an accident of evolution: a predator sponge that linked with its prey. Father was nothing but his victims. And when I had absorbed and cut him off from all of his victims, Father was nothing more than so much seaweed.

I was Father now. I contained within me all the knowledge of a hundred intelligent races. But I was still Toomin. The Ellimist. I was not content to live here, in this blue moon's seas. I was born a creature of flight, of open skies.

I opened my eyes and gazed out through the sea. Out over Father's hideous crop of the dead.

I released the tentacle that held me. It took a long time. Tendrils had penetrated me, entered my brain. There was pain, physical pain that I had not felt in decades. And when I was almost free I nearly drowned. The tentacle had supplied all my needs for food and air and had preserved me from aging.

Now I strangled, my lungs seized, my stomach heaved. I moved muscles that had not moved in a lifetime.

I kicked free of the tentacle, free! I opened my wings and flew slowly upward through the water, rose to the surface. Air!

Free! My face out of the water, untethered, free!

Could I fly? Could I possibly fly? How to get my wings above the surface? Impossible. Im —

It came like a tidal wave. A roaring waterfall of sights, sounds, images, ideas, emotions. Overwhelming. I was swept away by it, a free flyer in a hurricane.

All the minds I had downloaded into mine, they were all there, all crowded now into my own limited Ketran brain. I was a computer running a thousand sims at once. My own body seemed to exist in infinite variations. I had hands, feet, wings, tentacles, stingers, prods, claws, feelers; I had eyes of every kind, I could see light all across the spectrum, I could see X rays and cosmic rays and microwaves; I had ears to hear only the deepest bass notes, and ears to hear only the highest pitches, and ears to hear a fuzzball floating on a breeze at a thousand yard's distance.

And all of it, all those sense memories, all crammed into my own inadequate body and brain.

I fought down the rush, the deluge. I surfaced again, me, Toomin, the gamer who called himself Ellimist. I was in control. No, not control. No. All I could do was suppress the waiting onslaught. I couldn't use it. Couldn't open the door to it and use it without being overwhelmed.

I swam, scared now, staggered by what I had done, lost. I swam beneath the bright glowing disc of the planet above, beneath the white and brown moon, beneath the warmth of the distant sun.

I swam for a long time, but I was not lost. We had often used this moon of Father's as a game board, Father and I. I knew where each little island lay and in a few exhausting hours I lay prostrate on soggy soil.

After a while I opened my wings to the breeze and let them dry. The riot in my head was still there, still clamoring. A mob held at bay by flimsy gates.

When I was dry I took to the air. I flew for the first time in so long that I could not help but cry. I flew on the lift of my own wings, above the almost-endless sea, above the awful crop of the dead that still lay tethered to Father.

They were deteriorating now, of course. Father no longer kept them safe from age and the rotting effects of the water. He no longer nourished them.

They had reached their final deaths. The entire moon was a graveyard.

I flew and searched. I had never seen the place I was looking for but I knew it existed. Father had let us play across the surface of his world, but there had been blank zones, areas that simply never appeared. What secrets were there in those concealed redoubts?

I flew and caught a nice tail breeze. I was hungry. Amazing! I was tired. Wonderful! I was free.

Alone.

Ahead I saw the outlines of what I had expected to find. A hidden island. Larger than the rest and higher. It was dry compared to the other lands of this moon. It was thickly covered with vegetation, mostly green with some startling swatches of orange and red.

Here and there, nestled between the trees, were spacecraft. Some had been there so long they were completely overgrown with vines and moss and trees. Some looked like they might have crashed just weeks or at most months before.

They were huge, and they were small. Dangerous-looking and innocuous. Some bristled with weapons or were painted fantastically. Others were utilitarian boxes.

All the ships of all the races that had been lured to Father over the millions of years he lay in wait. I had found Father's trash dump.

It took a while but I located the Explorer. And I found the Searcher. Searcher was a crumpled, twisted mess. I landed on an undamaged spar and stood there a while.

The gravestone of my people. The last Ketran now stood vigil at the gravestone of his race.

Explorer was in better condition. It lay upside down, which was an inconvenience in gravity, but the engines powered up, and the systems worked. She would fly. I could leave Father's moon.

And go where?

I was now as alien as it is possible to be. The only Ketran in a galaxy that, with few exceptions, had never known we existed.

And I was an alien who contained within himself a multitude. I was filled up with answers to the questions of tens of thousands of relatives and friends on a thousand worlds. I knew where their loved ones had gone, why they had never returned. I was all that was left of Ket, but I was at the same time all that was left of other long-extinct races and of tribes and families.

I had become a living repository of life in a hun-

dred variations. Life that would remain closed behind the locked doors of my own feeble brain unless . . . unless I could become something else.

"You were right, Menno. We must adapt, in the
end. Adapt or die."

chapter 20

It took thirty more years to do all I needed to do.

I went through each ship, each wreck, and took what I could use. I burned roads through the jungle and built haulers. I built a sprawling shop with tools that would have made Jicklet drool with envy.

I dipped into the mass of minds that lived within me. Over time I learned to survive the storm of the multitude, to take what I needed and go on. Jicklet was often there with me. And an engineer named Hadra 232. And a Z-space theorist named Nu. And a hundred other scientists, technicians, theorists, builders, designers, innovators.

And biologists as well. Lackofa was with me. Others, many others, from other races.

The work changed shape, mutated, grew like a living thing and in fact became a living thing. For although I was building a ship, I was building so much more. I was building a new race. A race of one. A race of millions.

I was singular and plural all at once. I was alive and I was a machine. Engines were a part of me. Computers linked directly with my brain and soon the link was forgotten and the line disappeared. Sensors were my senses. I was vast. Vast enough to release the multitude.

Thirty years, and at last I was ready. I had passed most of a century on the blue moon. It was dying. The air worsened slowly, but that was all right; I no longer needed air. The waters reeked of decay, but I no longer needed to drink. The fish had long since become extinct. But I had saved the dead. And now I opened wide the gate to my multitude, never to close it again.

All my Ketrans, all my Generationals, my Daank-ins, my Hayati, my 333's, my Wurbs and Breets and Gofinickiliasts, my Multitudinals, my Chan Wath, my Skrit Na and Illamans and Capasins and my one Unemite and so many others. Race after race. I emptied each dead mind into my extended brain, my biological-mechanical-synthetic construct, all free again.

So much knowledge, so much. And yet, when the flood was calmed, only I was truly alive. It was all me. I was still alone.

I lit my engines and rose from the surface of the dying moon.

From space I looked back on it. What was fitting? Some races burned their dead, some ate them, some buried them in the ground. Some finality was called for so that the floating bones and exoskeletons and shells of all those honored dead could cease to be grotesque.

I called on my weapons and I blasted the moon till it broke apart, till the atmosphere was ripped away, till the sea boiled up into the vacuum, till the molten remains spiraled slowly down in the gravity well of the planet and were incinerated on reentry.

Then I entered Z-space and put a billion miles between myself and that foul place.

Now what was I to do? I was unique. As alone as only a unique creature can be. I was part of no species. I was part of many species, but there was no hope of companionship there. Who would welcome me into their system? I had become a physical embodiment of the inter-species uninet I used to dream of. I was a library of information from many races. And with my extended body/ship I was powerful beyond reckoning.

Now what?

Now what?

Now what? What is your game now, Ellimist?

I thought of returning to Ket. But that would only cause me pain. Return to what? To empty skies where my people once lived?

I flew. In and out of Z-space, in and out of orbits. Time meant nothing to me, I was in no hurry. But the loneliness was another matter. I took refuge in creating subroutines, simulations of people. I tried to talk to them, tried to . . . But how can you really talk to your own creation? How can you talk to a machine you've programmed? It's an exercise in narcissism. It's the beginning of madness.

I knew now why Father had kept me alive. He had long since learned the emptiness of communication without hope of surprise. A Ketran — any sentient species — is only his free will. Freedom and sentience are inseparable. The captive, programmed mind is no mind at all.

I flew for a long time. Years. Looking. For what? I didn't know.

And then, I dropped from Z-space and entered a system where two planets were at war.

They were technologically advanced, though not capable of Z-space travel yet. They communicated by microwave and laser emissions. They moved across the lands and seas and through the skies of their respective planets. They had suppressed most diseases.

Two planets in strangely close proximity, no more than a quarter million miles separating them at their closest points. One was called Jall, the other the Inner World. The Inner World was actually in the more distant orbit, but then "inner" may have been a reference to some other factor. Neither Jallians nor Inners were part of my multitude, though the 333's had knowledge of their existence. I was in a far reach of the galaxy.

I arrived, invisible to either side. I arrived in the midst of a ship-to-ship battle. In fact, I dropped out of Z-space within twenty miles of being struck by a terrifically powerful Jallian beam that missed its intended target, missed me, and finally, diffused and harmless, slightly warmed the nickel-and-iron surface of a passing asteroid.

"Well, well," I said. (I'd long since lost any reluctance to converse with myself.) "I seem to have stumbled into a war."

The Jallian ship, a fantastically painted behemoth half a mile long, fired again. This time the beam found its victim. A small, swift Inner ship that looked, with its smooth, swept lines as if it had been designed to move through water, blew apart.

The Jallian jubilation was short-lived. A swarm of Inner craft emerged from the primitive stealth-state that allowed them to hide from Jallian sensors.

The Jallian ship fired again and again and annihilated five of the attackers, nearly a third of the total. But then the Inners fired. Their weapons were weaker. The Jallian ship did not blow apart. But the outer skin had been sliced open. Pressurized atmosphere blew out into space. And bodies, too. Writhing figures, helpless.

I acted before thinking. Acted on pure instinct. I extended a force field between the Jallian ship and the Inner Worlders. Both sides fired. Neither side's weapons penetrated my force field.

I moved closer and let them see me. How it must have shocked them! Their ships were boxes of steel and titanium and composites. Mine was a living thing: crystal and flesh and composites all melded together, all wrapped in force fields of unchallengeable power. I was a visitor from a future they had only barely begun to glimpse.

By all rights they should have powered down and waited to learn my pleasure. Far from it. Both sides took less than five minutes to touch me with their active sensors, to feel around me, half-sighted.

And then the Inner Worlders opened fire. On me! The Jallians used the distraction to fire on the Inners, and in seconds what had been a two-front war became a three-way free-for-all.

I almost laughed. But the sheer malevolence of these two species was disgusting. I could have destroyed both fleets with a shrug of my wings.

I stretched out my power and wrapped my fields

around them. I drained their power, damped their engines, scrambled their sensors, and left them drifting, helpless through space.

Then I opened communications.

"Your war is over," I announced.

chapter 21

Two sets of furious faces appeared to me. The Jallians were represented by a multi-armed slug of sorts. She had no name, only a title, a designation. She was Life-giver of the Jain Sea. And indeed she was giving birth as she appeared to my enhanced sight. One after another, small, squirming grubs slid gooey and red from slits arranged in a circle around her middle. The grubs were picked up and carried away by attendants — the type of creatures I'd seen writhing in vacuums just moments earlier.

Life-giver of the Jain Sea was enraged. "Who are you, nothing, to interfere with me? I speak to a nothing! Obey me!"

She spoke a strange language, but with the database I had available there were few languages not immediately understandable to me.

The Inner Worlders had a more pleasing appearance, at least to my sensibilities. For one thing, they were winged, and I had the Ketran prejudice in favor of the flighted. And they had multiple, bright yellow eyes. The one who spoke for them called himself Captain Whee, which had a certain whimsical sound to me.

Captain Whee was polite, but still managed to convey hostility. "Stranger, please stand away. We have business with the Jallian vermin."

"I am unwilling to allow this slaughter to continue," I said mildly.

"This is not your concern," Captain Whee pointed out. "But we do admire your evident technological superiority. Were you to side with us and exterminate the Jallians, we would be happy to ally ourselves with you."

"That's a very gracious offer," I said dryly. "But I don't think there's going to be any exterminating."

"Nothing! Disappear, nothing! Avoid my notice!" the Life-giver roared. She could not believe that I refused to obey. It was an arrogance that was perhaps a function of her essential biology. Perhaps it is hard to remain humble when you are known as Life-giver.

But what was odd, what was surprising and disturbing to me, was my own emotional reaction: I was happy. I was talking to real, living creatures whose every word and motion were not mine to invent.

From the Jallian planet a second huge ship broke

from orbit and vectored at full speed toward us. Moments later the Inner Worlders responded with a virtual cloud of their small, sleek ships.

Were they intending to attack me or each other? Did it matter? Either was madness.

It was the game, all over again: Alien Civilizations. No different than any of the many scenarios Wormer or Inidar or Aguella and I had played.

The question was, How I should play it? I had already pulled a Menno: I had intruded into the game. Made myself a central player, onstage, rather than offscreen.

And yet I was still drawn to the subtler approach. What would either species learn if I simply annihilated their ships in a display of crude power? And was that really my place?

I did not ask myself whether it was my business to interfere at all. It was not that I confused game with reality. I simply saw these two objectionable species as fools trapped in a pointless hostility. Didn't I have the right to intervene? Of course I did.

I was not Menno, I was Toomin. I was Ellimist: the brilliant loser. But now I knew so much more. My wisdom was deep. My powers were vast. Surely . . . and then there was the core fact that I was not playing against anyone. No opponent, just the game itself.

The minimal move, then.

If this were really a game I would simply alter the orbits of the two planets so that they did not pass so closely. Slow them down or speed them up to matching, opposite orbits. Put their sun between them. They lacked the technology to fight a war across those distances.

But great as my powers were, they were not that great. And yet I could surely move an asteroid. Or two. Or a hundred.

The system's asteroid belt was just beyond the orbit of Inner World. It was a simple calculation, well within my abilities. And I had sufficient brute power in my body/ship.

I left the two sides to murder each other and withdrew to the asteroid belt. It would take some time: Asteroids are not rocks to be casually flung about. But perhaps the two sides, seeing what I was about, would suspend their battle.

I used my body/ship to nudge an asteroid, not a large one, out of its orbit. My engines were more than capable. The asteroid slid down the gravity well, vectored to find a new, lower, faster orbit.

I worked and waited. In a few weeks' time the two battling worlds had separated by enough to force them to suspend hostilities — a natural part of their conflict. It was only at their nearest approach that the two worlds could reach out and kill the other.

I waited as my fleet of asteroids hurtled through space. And when the time came I slowed them, braked, nudged them into place. It took the better part of a year.

And now the two planets were approaching convergence again, and I could see the war preparations in full swing: ships refitting and topping off their fuel.

I waited till the two worlds were just edging into battle range. And then, one by one, I blew the asteroids apart. Seventy-four asteroids of differing sizes became tens of thousands of meteors of every size. They were a dense, deadly cloud of projectiles that with each orbit would rip up anything that launched from either planet.

The Jallians and Inner Worlders would be unable to reach each other at least till such time as they developed vastly more capable spacecraft.

I had created an impenetrable orbital minefield.

The Jallian war with the Inner Worlders was over. And I had found my mission, my purpose in the galaxy.

chapter 22

It was as if the galaxy had conspired to make sense of my disjointed, fractured, bizarre life.

I had been a wastrel Ketran gamer. I had been a survivor of mass destruction. I had been a Z-spaceship captain. I had been a helpless captive, forced to be a new type of gamer. I had evolved into something the galaxy had never seen before, a melding of many technologies, the minds of many civilizations, all flowing in and through a matrix of music.

And now that strange resume seemed to match perfectly with a job that needed doing. I would be a peacemaker. And more: I would foster the growth and advancement of species. I would teach them the ways of peace. The massacre of my own people by the Capasins would not be repeated on any other world. Not so long as I was present!

I flew Z-space, emerged here and there, searching the galaxy, using every bit of my vast trove of knowledge to look, to see, to feel, to learn, to understand. I listened to the music of evolution itself, or so I flattered myself.

Life was everywhere. A thousand thousand

planets teeming with life. Most of it very primitive, but why should that stop me? I could step in early, I could "intrude," in Menno's phrase. And yet, I would intrude with exquisite sensitivity and the purest motivations. I would create harmonies. Boldness allied with restraint and a minimalist aesthetic, all in the service of moral certainties: that peace was better than war, that freedom was better than slavery, that knowledge was better than ignorance.

Oh, yes, the galaxy would be a wonderful place under my guidance.

I flew from star to star, world to world. Here I lifted up a failing race; there I ended a plague; in another place I fed the hungry. A century flew past. And another, and more and more. Time was almost meaningless to me now. My challenges were vast and worthy, they kept my mind engaged. I made friends on many worlds, became an honorary member of a hundred families, clans, tribes, species, races. They spoke of me, of the Ellimist as I had become known, with respect, gratitude, awe.

And then the day came that I happened by sheer coincidence to find myself within a relatively short distance of the scene of my first triumph. A thousand years had passed since I had stopped the war of Inner Worlders and Jallians.

Finding myself so near, I returned to savor. To reminisce.

I returned to find no signs of life on the Jallian world. The planet was sterile, its atmosphere almost gone.

The Inner World still teemed with life, but I caught no sign of microwave or radio or laser emissions. No satellites orbited the planet. The Inner Worlders were reduced in numbers and existing at a primitive technological level.

It took only a short while for me to reconstruct what had happened. It was easy enough once I found a single, still-orbiting mine. A primitive device, produced in great numbers by the Inner Worlders. They had launched huge numbers of them, laid them in the path of the onrushing Jallian world. Many of the mines had been annihilated by my meteor cloud. But many had survived, and then survived reentry to explode on contact with the surface of the Jallian planet.

Even now, a thousand years later, the radiation could be read. Even now the craters could be seen from space.

Morbidly I went about the work of compiling every detail. More than seven hundred impacts. Seven hundred nuclear explosions.

"Not such an easy game to win, is it?"

For a moment I thought the voice was my own. The tone of sarcasm and deprecation mirrored my own self-directed rage. But then my sensors lit up. Something was emerging from Z-space. Something big.

I spun, readied my defenses, still confident that nothing, no matter how unexpected, could really challenge me.

But the ship that appeared suddenly in normal space was nothing I had ever seen. Nothing that any of my multitude had ever seen.

This ship was not a ship: It was a planetoid, large enough to be a small moon. And yet it was Z-space capable. Incredible! Impossible! An illusion, it had to be.

I swept the planetoid with my sensors and I could literally feel the entity's acquiescence. It invited me to look. It did not care. It did not fear me.

There were life-forms on the planetoid, perhaps twenty thousand, in a wide array of species, most naturally evolved, but some, I suspected, were experimental. Created.

But there was only one life-form that truly concerned me: My sensors showed lines of power, raw, snapping power connecting this one creature to all the other life-forms.

I had not felt fear in so long . . . I almost did not recognize the emotion. Fear. I feared nothing! I was the Ellimist. In a thousand years I had not encountered anything, anyone to challenge me.

"The Ellimist," the creature said with a laugh I heard deep in my mind. "I have seen your handiwork in many places through this galaxy. I am pleased to meet you at last. I've been looking for you."

I could not see him; he hid his face from me.

"You know my name," I said, trying to conceal any slight sign of fear or agitation.

"Oh, but you're famous in so many places. The Great Cosmic Do-gooder."

"You have the advantage of me," I said. "I do not know you."

Then he showed himself to me. I saw with a shock that he was like me: As much machine as biological. But his biology was entirely different. He was evolved for the surface, or perhaps even for a subterranean life. No wings would ever lift those massive, muscled limbs. And no creature with that single, dominating red eye could ever navigate easily in three dimensions.

"I am called Crayak. Of course, that's just my game name." He laughed a knowing laugh, a ridiculing, belittling sound.

159

"You are a gamer?"

"Aren't we all?"

"No longer," I lied. "I no longer play a game. I do what I can to make this a better galaxy."

"Well, you've done a wonderful job of that here," Crayak said. "I can see plainly what happened: Your clever debris barrier gave them the idea of using nuclear mines. One planet destroyed the other, and, lacking a foe, lacking a challenge, the destroyer itself fell into barbarism and decay. Yes, quite a nice job."

It was true. There was no doubting it. Part of me wondered how it was that Crayak could read the signs so well. But mostly a single phrase went round and round in my head: brilliant loser. I had lost. With all the best of intentions, I had annihilated one species and reduced another.

I lost to Inidar, lost to Wormer, lost to Aguella. I had lost in a different way to Menno: By resisting his call for adaptation I had led the last of my people into Father's snare. And I had lost to Father, in the end, by becoming Father myself. What was I, after all, with all Father's victims contained within me? I was but a high-tech version of Father.

And now I had fallen victim to arrogance. I'd begun to believe in my own moral superiority. My own invincibility.

"You've been following me?" I asked Crayak.

"Yes." He waited. He knew what I wanted to ask, but he would make me ask it of him.

"How many others . . . like this?"

"Not many," Crayak said. "No, often you've succeeded admirably. Your solution to the Mamathisk self-annihilation game was brilliant. Subtle. Effective. You redirected them to a life of productive peace. I had to go in and destroy them myself."

I had begun to revive a little as he described my success. Then, his last statement.

"You did what?"

"I reversed the effects of your meddling," Crayak said. "The Mamathisk reverted to cannibalism when they experienced repeated crop failures. A plant parasite. Impossible for them to stop. But as you know, cannibalism is a losing adaptation. The Mamathisk are effectively extinct."

"Are you mad?!" I cried.

"No, I don't think so, Ellimist. I'm just a gamer. Like you. But with a perhaps different philosophy. I don't play the game to save the species, but to annihilate it. I play the game of genocide. This galaxy has even more potential games within it than the galaxy I left behind. I will cleanse this galaxy of all life, too. Then, when no sentient thing is left alive, I will kill you, Ellimist. That's my game. Shall we play?"

chapter 23

How many years, how many decades had I played Father's games? Losing every game. Until by sheer luck I found the game he could not win.

I couldn't afford to lose that way to Crayak. The game pieces had become real beings. We played for real lives. And I played the weaker side: I had to save; he had only to destroy.

And yet, here is the shameful truth: I needed Crayak as Father had needed me.

Crayak disappeared into Z-space and I followed him as well as anyone can follow another through that shifting nothingness. I found him waiting for me in a solar system with three inhabited planets. One of those worlds was the Capasin home world. I had avoided ever visiting the Capasin world. I didn't want to be tempted by notions of revenge.

Crayak had already been some days in the system. He had laid out his game pieces with terrifying ruthlessness.

"Here is the game, Ellimist: Three worlds. Each inhabited by a sentient race: Laga, the Folk, and the Capasins. I believe you may know of the Capasins.

There are three asteroids strategically placed. Three impacts within the next five minutes of time. Except that one of those asteroids has already been mined and will explode into harmless debris before it can hit — you have my word on that."

"The word of a mass murderer."

"Yes, but an honest murderer," he said, and laughed at his own wit. "You have time to reach and destroy one asteroid. Not the other two. If you guess wrong and destroy the mined asteroid then two planets will die. If you guess right and detonate one of the unmined asteroids, only a single world will die."

I wanted to rage, to curse the foul beast. No time! No time to cry foul; he would only laugh. Five minutes. Less now.

All data now! What did I know? The Capasin: civilized but extremely violent when they felt threatened — as they had upon receiving the earliest Ketran broadcasts. The Laga, subtechnological farmers. The Folk, not yet capable of spaceflight but technologically skilled and obsessed by a eugenic vision that motivated them to kill upwards of ninety percent of their own offspring for real or imaginary defects.

Where was that mine? That was the issue, not which species deserved to survive. The question was, which had Crayak chosen to spare? Would he save the species closest to his own values, or would he spare the least threatening? Which served his needs best: Capasins or the Folk? Who would he keep alive? And what would he expect me to do?

He would expect me to save the Laga. He would expect me to annihilate that asteroid and thus spare the peaceful farmers. And the Laga would be the species he hated most.

But, expecting me to save the Laga he would know that I would guess his mind.

What was the answer?

Seconds ticking. Time passing. I had to choose or make no play at all. Three massive asteroids twirled through black space, falling toward three planets.

I lit my engines, moved to position, and opened fire.

The Capasin asteroid heated, cracked, split. I fired again and again, shattering the remaining large chunks.

"Blow your mine!" I cried.

"As I agreed," Crayak said.

A huge explosion blossomed, a red fireball against black space. The explosion consumed what was left of the Capasin asteroid.

Wrong! I had guessed wrong!

I powered, full speed, to intercept the Laga asteroid. Fast! Faster! Too far to fire with any effect, fire anyway! I aimed, fired, watched my beams impact the distant asteroid. Too far away, and then the asteroid was within the shadow of the planet.

There are no shock waves in space. I did not feel the impact. But I could see the green and blue planet of the Laga shudder. An amazing, awesome, terrible sight. The planet shuddered. Seemed almost to stop, unimaginable momentum checked. Slowly at first, then faster, a crack appeared, many cracks. The land was ripped apart. The seas drained into these craters, into these chasms. The white hot core of the Lagan world met oceans of cold water and exploded with breathtaking violence.

The Lagan world blew apart in steam and fire and debris. Blew apart. A faint bluish haze of atmosphere clung to some of the larger chunks, then evaporated.

Every living creature died.

I had already turned away, already lit my engines, already calculated the utter impossibility, already knew my own impotence, raced for no reason, with no hope, raced and fired and missed, all the while knowing I did it for my own sanity and no other reason.

The Folk died more slowly than the Lagans. The asteroid struck a glancing blow. It shocked the planet, ripped away a continent-sized chunk, and flew on past. The damaged planet wobbled wildly. Every structure on the planet was flattened, every sea-shore drowned, every lake spilled, millions died.

And yet the Folk lived on.

"Their orbit is badly destabilized," Crayak observed. "You can see that they will slip slowly, then faster, wobbling, torn by shattering earthquakes, slide down and down the gravity well, atmosphere boiling away, suffocating, a few surviving in trapped pockets of air till of course they are roasted alive by their own sun."

"Some of them can still be saved!" I cried.

"Yes. And you can stay here and save them, Ellimist. Or you can follow me to the next game. Save a few of these creatures, or perhaps save entire worlds. Your choice. It's all a part of the game."

chapter 24

The next game.

And the next.

Game after game, if you could call these blood-baths games. Each time I played catch-up, always the beast Crayak was there before me, always he controlled the playing field.

His powers were greater than mine. He toyed with me. Mocked and ridiculed me. Worlds died and the galaxy grew emptier and years passed, centuries, millennia, and always I saved only a few, never all.

I could never find the winning move. My concern for the innocent wouldn't let me walk away. Or was it just my ego?

There had to be another way. I had beaten Father after a long while. There had to be another way.

How had I beaten Father? By possessing a talent he lacked. But music would not stop Crayak.

At last I lit my engines in the wreckage of yet another planet and escaped into Zero-space with Crayak's triumphant howls in my ears.

No more. No more game. Not until I found a way.

I flew for a long time, longer than I had ever stayed in Zero-space before. I emerged finally at a far edge of the galaxy, billions of light-years from the populated core of old systems and old planets.

Out here the skies were darker. Out here even my sensors could not pick up radio or microwave emissions. There was silence out here. Was there even life?

I surveyed planets and found life, often simple single-celled life, but here and there more advanced forms. On one world I discovered true sentience: a simple, primitive species barely at the dawn of civilization.

I had been in space for millennia now. Thousands of years had passed since I had defeated Father. Thousands more years since I had last encountered another free, rational, equal being — aside from Crayak, and could he be called rational?

I was lonely, desperately lonely.

I no longer had a body in any true sense of the word. I was vastly more machine than creature. And now, in the depths of despair, with disillusion poisoning my mind, with a crushing sense of my own weakness, haunted by guilt, I craved the simplicity and comfort of companionship.

I wanted a body. I wanted to go down to the planet below and fly or at least walk free.

It was not difficult, not really. I dispatched one of my drones down to the surface to take a sample of DNA from the sentient creatures down there. With that DNA sample I easily grew a replica body.

The harder question was how I might inhabit that form. There was no chance, no possibility of using the creature's own biological brain to store all that I was. My own brain contained hundreds of times the data capacity of that simple organ.

How to carry myself into the creature? I would have to edit my data. Reduce it down to what mattered most: the ideas, facts, images, memories that were most vital.

It would mean that, for a while at least, there would be two of me. The complete unabridged Ellimist, and a sort of sketch of myself.

I spent a year deciding what should and what should not be placed into the limited biological creature I'd cloned. It was a wonderful year. A year of learning. For what could be more deeply educational than poring over all you know and deciding what truly matters?

In the end what I placed inside the creature was me. Toomin. The Ketran gamer.

I kept the child me. Strange, but all these years later, all these battles later, it was Toomin I valued most.

I brought Aguella's memory: my one great love. And I carried Lackofa with me, too, for his skepticism, his integrity, and his sense of humor.

And to my surprise I found I could not do without Menno. Rebellion, too, was something I needed.

I took sketch memories, overviews without detail, intuitions. Strange, but I did not wish to edit out all the terrible things. I could not allow myself to remove the destruction of my home world, or the disaster of crashing the Explorer, or my long captivity under Father. I could not even bring myself to edit Crayak.

But at last I was done. I poured this abbreviated version of myself into the brain of the clone and all at once I was alive in two places, in two forms simultaneously.

I looked at myself as my new self looked at me. With eyes and ears and deep-probing sensors I observed the biological me: I was a strong beast standing firmly on four hooved legs. I had a slender upper body, not so much different from my own Ketran torso, but with only two arms and no wings at all.

The four eyes were familiar but on this creature evolution had invented the wonderful device of movable stalks so that two of the eyes could be aimed in divergent directions.

I had shaggy blue-and-tan fur and a tail weapon of limited utility. I ate by running, by crushing grasses within my hollow hooves and digesting bulk and nutrients. I had no mouth.

At the same time I looked at the older, fuller me, the machine-spacecraft me, through two large eyes and two stalk eyes. I seemed vast and overwhelming and complex. I, the new, biological me, stood on an open platform, sheltered only by a force field that held space at bay. The old me was a machine, there was no denying that. I could still see a wizened, aged, desiccated Ketran enmeshed in the gears, so to speak, but the soaring crystal spars and titanium machines and composite engine housings and weapons systems extended now for a mile or more.

It made me sad, somehow, to really see myself from the outside. In my mind's eyes I was still a Ketran male. To any other eye I was a terrifying device of unrivaled power.

The me that was the clone flew down to the planet.

I landed in a wild, untamed wilderness of tall blue grass and fantastically colored trees. I sent my shuttle back into orbit and tried out my legs.

Wonderful! With each step I tasted the earth. My nose filled with the scents of flowers, filled my brain. It had been so long since I had smelled anything. The body was supple, swift, strong. The tail could be used to stab at anything approaching me from behind.

I was no fool; I knew this tail meant there were predators in this ecosystem, but I was not overly concerned. I carried a small beam weapon strapped around my waist and adapted for my physical hands.

I walked through the forest, pushing and grunting my way through dense thickets, shouldering aside clumps of grass that would suddenly adhere together and become a virtual wall.

I had a goal. I had surveyed the planet and knew it well. I emerged from the forest into openness, a field where the grass had been hacked down to form a sort of rough lawn.

Simple habitations had been created by scooping out shallow bowls in the ground and half-covering them with graceful thatched roofs.

I stepped into the open. Three of my "fellow" blue-tan creatures were within a hundred yards. Their reaction to me was instantaneous. They charged me at top speed, surrounded me, and twisted around awkwardly to aim their pointed tail blades at me.

Three stubby blades quivered nervously within a few feet of my vulnerable throat.

Not quite the welcome I'd been hoping for.

chapter 25

I held up my hands, palms out, to show that I carried no weapon and meant no harm. But of course this gesture was less meaningful when dealing with a species that carried its weapon in its tail.

The three creatures flashed a series of complex hand signals at one another. If I'd had my full multitude with me I'd have been able to instantly decipher this gestural language. But I was a more limited me. I could guess but no more.

I decided to try and copy some of the gestures. The creatures watched but were quickly frustrated. Evidently I was speaking gibberish.

And now it was becoming more clear that the three were discussing whether or not to kill me outright as a dangerous stranger. Two of them were quite intent on this and made wild, angry gestures. They cavorted, rose on hind legs, and darted their hindquarters toward me, stabbing the air with their tail blades.

The third, a smaller creature with restless stalk eyes and contrastingly calm main eyes, restrained them, but only with difficulty.

I could sense quite clearly their emotional states. It wasn't just the body language. They seemed capable of projecting a sort of basic emotional language by some means I could not discern.

<I'm not an enemy,> I said. I said it without thinking, automatically accessing my communications system — a system that was part of my other body, no part of this form.

And yet, I saw a subtle relaxation on the part of the creatures. They had "heard" me. Or had at least heard the emotional tone.

I tried again. <I wish to be a friend. I am here to . . . > I was about to say that I was there to help. But no, that wasn't it anymore. <I am here to learn from you.>

More rapid hand gestures. Emotions cooled. And then, very suddenly, all three of them spun. I was forgotten. Something was coming from the forest across the clearing. Something large.

It walked on six legs, each as thick as a tree trunk, a knuckling walk. It had a low-slung head that swung from side to side as it walked. The beast was armored with clunky, leatherish plates all down its back.

It was huge but would not have seemed like any sort of threat had I not seen the reactions of the blue creatures. They clearly saw it as a danger. The emotion was all too easy to feel.

Then the beast began to move and I reciprocated their emotion. I would never have believed something so big could move so fast.

More of my fellow blue quadrupeds appeared, rushing up from all angles, racing to cut the monster off before it could reach the cluster of scoops. My three companions attacked as well, headlong, heedless.

I followed at a tearing speed, my hooves kicking up clods of dirt as I ran. The first of my "brothers" reached the monster. The beast killed two effortlessly. It paused to eat, to rip the two martyrs apart and swallow them, all but ignoring the brave stabs of their fellows.

It was a sadly one-sided battle. And I should have stayed out of it. I had not come to fight. But I was, physically at least, one of these creatures, and there would be very little of the companionship I craved, very little learning, very little relaxation so long as they were being massacred.

I drew my handheld beam weapon and shot the monster in the head. It died and fell in a heap.

From that day on I was a welcomed, revered member of the tribe.

They had no name for their race, no special gestural label for their species, only hand-words for their tribe. As far as they were concerned, their planet was irrelevant, their species a useless abstraction. They were this tribe, this group, and no more.

It was I who came up with the hand-word for their race and, for the benefit of my own word-oriented brain, a spoken name as well.

I named them Andalites.

I lived with the Andalites for many years. Happy years, by and large. They were primitive people. Their gestural language consisted of fewer than two hundred words or phrases. They had no art, no science, no agriculture. But they had already evolved from pure grazers, herd members, into distinct individuals. They had potential.

I lived with them, and refused to teach, refused to interfere. On one other occasion I employed my weapon to fend off a monster's attack. But that was all. Aside from that I was an Andalite, concerned with keeping the fire going, with maintaining the roof of my little scoop, with carefully avoiding over-feeding in dry weather, with tending the trees so they would drop their delicious leaves at harvest time, with all the simple minutiae of daily life.

Most of all, I had friends. I "spoke" with living beings who spoke back, not with the canned, programmed, expected responses of computers or dead memories, but with the wonderful unpredictability of life.

I was no longer lonely. I no longer bore the weight of the galaxy on my inadequate shoulders.

From time to time I would return to my other self in orbit and download all my new experiences and memories. That other me was grateful, eager. That other me savored every detail. Felt the warmth of closeness. A warmth denied me since the death of Aguella and Lackofa.

I married.

Her name was Tree. The Andalites only used a dozen or so names — Tree, Water, Star, Grass, and so on. Probably twenty percent of the females in the tribe were named Tree.

We had a child: Star. But Star died soon after birth of a disease that attacks the Andalite young.

I had watched entire worlds die. I had lost my own race. How could I care so much about this one small, unsteady creature? How could her death cut me so deeply?

The pain was awful. Unbearable. And yet I was glad to learn that I could still feel.

The disease that had killed her was easily curable. The orbiting me took only a few seconds to discover the pathogen and work out simple countermeasures. I had the power to keep any Andalite child from dying of that disease. I could ensure that no other Andalite parent would ever experience that same loss.

I had the power.

I had the power to do it all: to eliminate predators, to wipe out disease, to ensure an adequate food supply, to biologically alter the Andalites so that they . . .

I had that power. I had used that power before, and ended up annihilating worlds.

And yet, how could I not? How could I not wipe out disease? How could I not stop evil?

"You hide here among these primitive creatures," I berated myself. "You cower and run from Crayak and do nothing to stop him. You want to solve the easy problems and avoid the larger ones? Is that your morality, Toomin the Ellimist?"

Tree came to me and made the hand-words for "child."

"You want to have another child?" I signed back, incredulous.

"Yes."

"But another child may die, too, my wife."

"Yes."

"Then why have another child? If not the disease, then the monsters, or a famine. Why have another child?"

"Disease take one," Tree admitted. Then, with growing defiance, "Monster take one. Famine take one. More children, some live."

I had another child. And this one did not fall prey to the illness. We named him Flower.

By the time Tree died of old age Flower had become a leader of the tribe. His sister Grass was married herself. Their two siblings, Sky and Water, died. Three of our five children had died, two had lived.

As I helped bury Tree's body according to the ritual that would allow her spirit to strengthen the grass, I knew my time with the Andalites was over.

I had gone there making sanctimonious noises about learning, never really expecting to learn anything new. And yet from these primitive, precivilized creatures I had learned how to defeat, or at least resist, Crayak.

More children, some live.

For every race Crayak exterminated, I would plant two new ones.

chapter 26

A hundred thousand generations passed and I had seeded life on as many worlds. I was growing "children" faster than Crayak could exterminate them. My travels, and the database of my multitude, had left me with an encyclopedic knowledge of habitable worlds and systems. And in some cases I simply created habitable worlds where only barren land had been: Melting ice caps to release water was one method, introducing oxygen-producing plant species was another.

I had the advantage now. Crayak had to try to find my new species, simple peoples who did not announce their presence with radio emissions. Primitive species hiding amidst the billions of planets.

And, for the first time, I grew a wholly new species. They were invented in my body/ship, created of bits and pieces of DNA. I accented their intelligence. I quashed their aggressiveness.

I called them Pemalites.

To the Pemalites I gave technology. They became an advanced species within a few decades of my creating them. As their creator, I gave them laws:

They would never practice violence, and they would conceal their existence as long as possible.

And I gave them a mission: to carry life everywhere.

With all my powers I still could not equal the volume of work done by the Pemalites. They took to the stars in a cloud of ships, carrying plant and animal species with them as they went. They spread life like a benign contagion.

Not even Crayak could find them all. Nor even a fraction of them all. Life was winning the race against death. Good was outrunning evil.

In all that time, millennia, I had not encountered Crayak. But eventually we must meet.

It happened without warning. I emerged from Z-space in a previously unvisited solar system. A massive jolt hit me before I could so much as switch on my sensors. An energy beam of shocking power.

For a split second I was simply overwhelmed. Every system flickered. Every synapse and connection stuttered. It was a blow that would have killed me ten thousand years earlier.

But I was no longer quite the creature I'd been when Crayak had last seen me. I had followed the same theory for my own survival as I had for the survival of life itself: I had grown, replicated, expanded.

I had broken "myself" into several dozen separate

semibiological ships. I was three dozen crystal/ships, all connected, all united by real-time communications on several different levels at once: everything from simple microwave and laser to more subtle connections based on mind-crystal harmonics.

Crayak's assault annihilated three of my portions. But that was less than a tenth of what now constituted the Ellimist.

Crayak still inhabited his dark, gloomy world. Still surrounded himself with sycophants and toadies. Still possessed the weapons and abilities he'd had. And now his power was not so much greater than mine. If at all.

"It seems I have survived," I said to him. "Let's see if you do as well."

I aimed and I fired with everything I had.

Crayak's dark planetoid staggered. Huge chunks, chunks the size of mighty mountains, exploded into space.

"You've grown," Crayak sneered.

"And you have not. Life has advantages over death."

"Only the most temporary advantages, Ellimist. Life is short. Death is eternal."

"You race from place to place, a fool trying to stamp out a contagion. You're too slow. Life has outrun you."

"Life, no. But you, Ellimist, yes, you have complicated my plans. So now, with deep regret, I must end our little game."

"I see. You lack the courage to play a game you might lose. A coward after all."

"A survivor, Ellimist."

He fired.

The battle was on. He fired, I fired. I threw nuclear missiles at him and replaced them swiftly — one of my "portions" contained an arms factory. The missiles exploded against his force field, sapping his power, dumping the radiation of a quasar down on him and his creatures.

He blazed at me with gravity distorters that twisted and turned space itself and bent and broke me.

I struck back with countermeasures to blind and confuse him. And then Crayak turned and ran.

No. He would not escape me. I was going to follow him, hunt him down, and annihilate him.

I chased him into Zero-space. We carried our battle into another system. The two of us orbited a massive star and sucked the energy from it to keep hacking away at each other. We hurled asteroids, we warped the form of space itself, we stabbed at each other with energy beams.

Crayak ran again. And I followed him. The taste

of victory was in my mouth, the hunger for revenge and vindication.

I struck at him with beams of energy powered by a star. Unimaginable force. I missed and struck a planet and vaporized an ocean. The species that inhabited that world would not last more than a year on their damaged world.

But there was no time to stop. I told myself I would make it all right when Crayak was dead. I told myself I would come back when Crayak was gone once and for all.

But it was I who ran from the next battle. And the next. Crayak had learned from me. He added to his own powers and so did I.

He ran. I chased. I ran. He chased. And as the battle raged through normal space and Zero-space we each grew. That was the strange paradox of it: We each grew stronger. Each more deadly. Each more accomplished at inflicting pain and damage on the other.

We had become symbiotic at some level. Neither of us could kill the other, neither of us could pull away because now, now after so much time, now the other was even stronger.

The destructive power we now employed annihilated solar systems in their entirety. Civilizations that had barely raised their heads to look at the stars were obliterated. Advanced worlds, arrogant with their space travel abilities watched, helpless, stunned, and were annihilated.

Still Crayak and I grew stronger and more deadly, but if anything, it was I who grew most dangerous now.

There were two lines on a cosmic graph: One was the number of living planets, down and down. Life was failing around the galaxy as the two mad giants rolled here and there and crushed the helpless beneath them.

The other graph line, though, showed my own slow ascension over Crayak.

It was a hideous race to see which would happen sooner: my triumph over Crayak or our mutual destruction of all life in the galaxy.

And then, sheer accident took Crayak and me down a path neither of us had known existed.

Crayak laid a trap for me. He was desperate. Ready to gamble anything. So he began to move with a definable pattern. He deliberately laid the groundwork for me to guess his next move.

It worked. I read his pattern and foolishly ascribed it to exhaustion on his part. Thus it was that I emerged from Zero-space within a few hundred thousand miles of a force that neither I nor Crayak could hope to defeat: a black hole.

chapter 27

I now consisted of four thousand two hundred and twenty portions. I emerged from Zero-space trailing my vast, extended body behind me. The instant I emerged I saw the trap.

Too late!

The pull of the black hole was impossible to fight. I had great power. I did not have this power. My most forward portions fell into that gravity well with no chance at all of escape.

Crayak had laid the trap to perfection.

I shot an order to my other portions: Do not emerge!

Milliseconds from final disaster the remaining parts of me cancelled their descent from Z-space. I was wounded, not killed. But oh, how I was wounded.

I watched helplessly as vast parts of me, including the remnants of the original ship/body, all that was left of the true Ketran me, fell toward that black hole.

I was everywhere at once, lost, turned, twisted. In Z-space, in real space far away as parts of me emerged randomly, and falling into the horrible crushing mouth of the black hole.

I was bits and pieces.

The pain! My connections were across so many levels. It was not just a data stream, it was more than that. Those were my arms and wings there, falling, diminishing, being crushed by gravity.

Those were my eyes and ears spread out through space and nonspace. Stretched.

I felt the connection break down, felt it as if parts of my body were being sawed off. Pain! My mind was closing in, collapsing, no! Fragments. Pieces of me. Distorted cries and shouts of wild disjointed communication.

The universe itself seemed to disintegrate. The stars fell apart, opened themselves up like blossoming flowers. And then . . . and then . . .

I seemed to float in a place like nothing I had seen or imagined. All around me I saw massive, twisted lines of pure power, snapping and color-shifting. I saw numbers, deluges of them, I could hear them roaring around my ears. I reached out a vast hand and could run it over the curves of space itself. I could stroke the very curves of space-time.

I saw . . . I saw everything, the inside, underside, inner, and outer of everything at once.

I lived still.

But where was I?

What was I?

I was within a black hole, within Zero-space, within real space and yet unified into one whole through a medium I could not yet conceive.

I was seeing, hearing, feeling in all places at once. The effect was extreme disorientation.

I tried instinctively to pull my parts together, but I could not. It was impossible that I should still be alive, impossible that I could flap wings that were still in Zero-space, impossible that I should seem to wiggle pods inside a black hole.

I was aware of Crayak, I felt him approach my real-space portions. He was attacking me piecemeal, exploding parts of me with great glee.

I felt physical parts of me evaporate, burned away by energy beams. And yet my mind was not diminished.

Portions of me were now fully within the black hole, they were crushed to dots, crushed to the size of atoms, destroyed for all intents and purposes.

And yet I lived.

Something was happening. Something . . .

One by one Crayak annihilated the component parts of me. Hundreds of them. Thousands of them. And when nothing was left of me in real space he chased me into Zero-space and squeezed those helpless, inanimate bits of machinery and flesh and crystal out into real space where they could be destroyed.

And still I lived.

How much time had passed? Unknowable. I was no longer within time. I could see time as a series of interwoven strands, a trillion trillion strands of possibility.

Was I dead? Was I in some sort of afterlife?

Dead, no. The dead do not see, and I saw! I saw things no living creature had ever seen before. I was deep within the structure of the universe, I was within the code of creation.

There was nothing left of me, nothing that anyone could see or touch. I was gone, and yet I lived.

END GAME

chapter 28

I don't know how long I floated through this eerie, brilliant, wondrous landscape of pure energy and purest beauty. Time was for other creatures. Time's arrow did not carry me along with it.

I knew nothing of this. I was a mere creature, for all my multitudes, for all my powers, I was, after all, a mere mortal creature.

It was as if one of the primitive Andalites I'd known had suddenly been thrust into the command center of a starship. I was an ignorant savage. An extreme primitive.

But I knew this: As simple and primitive as I might be, I could literally touch and move the vibrating lines of space-time.

Was I grown extremely big? Or had I shrunk to submolecular size? Size meant nothing. There was no size in this place.

I lived, and that was all I knew. I was alive without form, alive without synapses to fire, without food to devour, without limbs to control. I saw without eyes and tasted without tongue and moved with no wings or pods or engines to move me.

This I knew.

And I knew one other thing as well, a lesson hard-learned from millennia of war: My foe would find me.

An absurdly rare event, a cosmic coincidence had fashioned me. The odds? The odds were billions to one, trillions to one, incalculable.

But those were odds of this thing happening once. The odds of it happening again were great. Crayak learned. Crayak watched. Once I revealed myself to him, once I acted in such a way as to show myself, Crayak would find the way to follow me here. And as I was unchanged in mind and morality, so he would be unchanged.

Carefully, frightened at last into true humility, I began to study this new environment. I found I could see into the real world, see the events and peoples who made up these space-time strands.

They seemed to rise and mature and age and fall in the blink of an eye, and as I watched and studied and learned I knew that hundreds of thousands and finally millions of years were passing in real space.

I saw Crayak out there, still at his evil work. I saw lines go dark, unravel, coil up into nothingness as he massacred planets. Billions of lives become nothingness.

I had planted a great deal of life, and my Pemalites still lived to spread more, but the tide was turning once more in Crayak's favor.

At last, knowing I had so much more still to learn, knowing my own deep inadequacy, I struck back.

Crayak entered a system of nine planets orbiting a medium yellow star. Two of the worlds, a red planet and a blue, were populated. The red planet was already doomed, its atmosphere was oozing away, and Crayak could do no real harm there.

But the blue planet teemed with life. The dominant species type were huge, brutish beasts in a fantastic array of forms. Giant, slow-moving plant eaters and violent, rapacious killers with tearing teeth and deadly talons. There was intelligence there, but no sentience, I could see it so clearly.

Not in the great, domineering brutes, but in a handful of small, swift, fur-bearing prey animals did the future of this world lie.

They had only to be left alone and in forty or sixty million years there would emerge a great people.

Crayak saw none of his, he saw only that there was life there. He aimed his weapons at the blue planet and fired, and I drew gently on the fabric of space-time and his weapons struck nothing. The planet was gone, halfway around its orbit.

195

He tried again, and each time I applied my crude but powerful countermeasures.

And then, in confusion, Crayak withdrew to consider.

I knew he would be with me soon.

chapter 29

"So here you are, Ellimist."

"I've been expecting you, Crayak."

He appeared to me as he always had. As a dark monster. I knew how I appeared to him: I had mastered the simple trick of projecting myself in whatever guise suited me best. I appeared to him as a simple Ketran.

"Your advantage is gone, Ellimist."

"We are equals now," I agreed. "You can no longer harm me personally. You understand that?"

"I cannot harm you, Ellimist, but I can hurt you. I can kill the things you love."

"You can try, Crayak. But in the end you are a fool. Do you not see that everything you do I can undo? You can slaughter and I can reverse time itself to restore life. But I tell you this: If we carry on our war inside the bowels of space-time itself we will end by collapsing this universe and killing ourselves as well as every thing in it."

"It's a pointless game that has no winner," Crayak admitted. "But what else is there for the two of us?"

"We could watch. We could admire the advance of evolution."

"Unacceptable. I would choose my own destruction over that. To live for all of eternity as a passive observer? There must be a game. If there is no game there is nothing for me."

"Then let us play a game, Crayak."

"There will have to be rules."

"Yes, there will have to be rules."

"And a winner?"

"That, too, though it will take millions of years."

Crayak smiled his hideous smile. "I'm not going anywhere."

"Then come," I said, "let us play the final game."

Epilogue

I told the dying human, "Now you know who I am. What I am."

"Yeah. You were a kid. Like me in some ways, a kid who got in way too deep and couldn't get back out."

"A kid."

"You were trapped. You still are. I've been trapped."

"Yes," I said.

"Was I one of your game pieces? Were all six of us just game pieces?"

I considered that for a moment. Who is to say who is piece and who is player? How often had I wondered whether I myself was just a game piece in a still larger game whose players laughed at my pretensions?

"I did not cause you to be one of the six. You are . . . you were . . . a happy accident. An unwitting contribution from the human race to its own survival."

The human was silent. No begging, no pleading for life. At the end, acceptance came even to this strong, turbulent spirit.

"You said I could ask one more question."

"Yes."

"I can't ask if we win, I can't ask if it will all turn out okay."

"I don't know those answers."

"Okay, then answer this, Ellimist: Did I . . . did I make a difference? My life, and my . . . my death . . . was I worth it? Did my life really matter?"

"Yes. You were brave. You were strong. You were good. You mattered."

"Yeah. Okay, then. Okay, then."

A small strand of space-time went dark and coiled into nothingness.

A Deadly Visit from Old Friends

ANIMORPHS

K. A. Applegate

David is back and he wants revenge. With his new evil companions, he sets out to destroy the Animorphs. As if one deadly enemy isn't enough, an even darker force emerges onto the scene. Now the Animorphs won't only have to battle David, they will have to reckon with Crayak himself.

ANIMORPHS #48: THE RETURN

Coming to Bookstores this November

Watch ANIMORPHS on NICKELODEON TV

Visit the Web site at: www.scholastic.com/animorphs

Watch for the GTI game in fall 2000

ANIMORPHS®

K. A. Applegate

$4.99 US each!